I0622705

THE PAIN OF
ONKAI
後見

BY
N. K. EDO

PROLOGUE

THE VILLAGE SAT NESTLED in a cradle of mountains, untouched by the chaos that plagued the world below. Surrounded by towering cliffs and dense forests, it was a haven of peace, where the people lived quietly, their lives intertwined with the land. The air was crisp, the sounds of birds and running water a constant comfort to the villagers. For generations, they had known no war, no famine, no fear.

THE LEGEND OF ONKAI

It began with a shift in the wind—an unnatural stillness that settled over the valley like a shroud. The usual hum of life was replaced by an eerie silence, as though the world itself was holding its breath. The ground beneath the villagers' feet trembled, faintly at first, then stronger, until the quakes were undeniable. Pots rattled on shelves, animals grew restless, and a low, distant rumble echoed through the mountains.

They gathered outside their homes, faces turned upward in confusion and concern.

Then, through the mist that clung to the mountain pass, they saw it—a hulking, broad figure moving slowly but with purpose, each step reverberating through the earth. His form was monstrous, almost impossible to comprehend. The first thing they noticed were his arms, long and grotesque, ending in claws that dripped with a black, viscous ooze. Wherever it fell, the earth hissed and smoked, leaving smoldering craters in his wake. His skin, if it could be called that, was a patchwork of jagged, charred scales, blackened and cracked as though they had been scorched by fire. These scales caught the faint light, gleaming with an otherworldly sheen, each one a reflection of the pain he had caused and absorbed.

But it was his eyes that struck fear into the hearts of the villagers. Two burning orbs of hatred, glowing deep red, flickering like the flames of a forge. They did not simply look at the people—they bore into them, as if seeing their very souls. A chill ran through the crowd, and the first whispers of fear passed through their ranks.

"Demon..." someone breathed, the word barely a whisper but carrying the weight of dread. Mothers clutched their children closer, farmers gripped their tools as if they might offer some protection, and the

village elder stepped forward, his face pale but resolute.

Onkai stopped at the edge of the village, his massive
frame towering over the nearest homes. He stood still
for a moment, savoring the fear that radiated from the
people like a sweet perfume. The silence stretched,
thick and oppressive, as if the very air had grown
heavy with the weight of his presence.

And then, he smiled.

The corners of his mouth twisted upward, revealing
sharp, jagged teeth stained with the remnants of his
past victims. It was not a smile of joy or triumph—it
was the smile of a predator that knows its prey is
trapped, hopeless, and vulnerable. Slowly, deliberately, he lifted one of his massive arms, the black ooze
dripping from his claws in thick, heavy droplets. His
hand hovered above the nearest building, a humble
structure made of wood and stone, its walls trembling
as the ground shook beneath him.

With a single motion, Onkai brought his hand
down, smashing the building into splinters. The
sound was deafening, a thunderous crash that reverberated through the valley. The villagers screamed,
their fear breaking into panic as they scattered in all
directions. Some ran toward the forest, others toward
the mountains, but none could escape the terror that
had descended upon them.

Onkai's laughter rumbled like distant thunder, low and menacing. His eyes gleamed with delight as he watched the chaos unfold, savoring every scream, every plea for mercy. He did not chase them, not yet. He preferred to let them run, to feel the full weight of their fear before he crushed them. Pain, after all, was not a thing to be rushed.

The village was his now, and so too were their lives.

Onkai moved slowly through the village, each of his massive steps leaving deep, smoldering prints in the earth, the ground cracking and smoking beneath his weight. His presence was overwhelming, a shadow of death that loomed over every building, every terrified soul. His burning eyes flicked over the chaos, relishing the sight of people stumbling and falling in their desperate attempts to flee.

The village's narrow streets became a web of confusion. Parents cried out for their children, old men shouted warnings as they tried to usher others toward the forest, but it was futile. Onkai could sense their fear. He had all the time in the world.

A woman, clutching a small child in her arms, bolted toward the edge of the village. Her heart pounded in her chest, her feet barely touching the ground as she ran faster than she ever had before. The child sobbed, his tiny hands gripping her clothes. Just as she thought they might reach the tree line, she felt it—a searing heat behind her, like the breath of a furnace.

She turned, and there he was, towering over her, his eyes glowing with cruel amusement.

With a single motion, Onkai's clawed hand swept across the ground, sending the woman and child tumbling through the air. They landed hard in the dirt, dazed and wounded. The child whimpered as the mother tried to shield him, her body trembling. Onkai loomed over them, his smile widening as he raised his foot and brought it down.

The ground trembled, and a scream pierced the air briefly before being snuffed out—a sound that echoed through the village and sent a shudder of hopelessness through those still alive—a sound that would be repeated many times this day.

Onkai savored the moment, the heat of his breath rolling over the scattered survivors. They ran, yes—but there was no escape. Their fear clung to the air, thick and palpable, feeding him, making him stronger with every second. It was not enough to simply kill them; he had to see their despair, their broken hope, their suffering.

Onkai continued his slow march through the heart of the village, his path of destruction widening. Homes were torn apart with ease, the thick beams splintering under his claws as if they were twigs. Fires sparked from the destruction, catching on roofs and spreading quickly. Thick, black smoke billowed into the sky, choking the air and making it nearly impossible to see through the haze.

A group of villagers had gathered in the town's square, led by the village elder. His old face was pale, but his hands were steady as he gripped a simple wooden staff. Around him, men armed with makeshift weapons—axes, pitchforks, even sharpened stones—stood ready to fight. They knew their weapons were no match for the demon, but they had nowhere left to run.

Onkai noticed them, his smile fading into a snarl of contempt. He turned toward the square, his massive form casting a shadow over the armed villagers. They braced themselves, shouting war cries, their voices trembling but defiant. The elder stepped forward, staff raised as if he could ward off the beast with sheer will.

"You may kill us," the elder called out, his voice steady despite the fear in his eyes. "But you will not break us."

Onkai paused for a moment, considering the words. Then, with a swift and brutal motion, he lashed out with his clawed hand, sending a wave of black ooze flying through the air. It splashed across the ground and walls, sizzling and hissing as it corroded everything it touched. Several villagers screamed as the ooze landed on them, burning through skin and muscle in seconds. They collapsed, writhing in agony.

The elder stood frozen, his eyes wide as he watched his people die in the most horrific way. Onkai's deep laughter rumbled through the square. The demon moved forward, sweeping his arm through the air again, knocking aside those who still stood. The makeshift weapons clattered to the ground, useless.

The elder fell to his knees as Onkai approached. His voice, once strong, now shook as he whispered, "Please… spare them."

Onkai loomed over him, silent for a moment, his burning eyes boring into the elder's soul. Then, with a low growl, he reached down, his massive claws closing around the old man's frail body. The elder gasped, the air crushed from his lungs and his skin burned in the beast's fiery grip, but still he struggled, gripping his staff as if it could protect him. Onkai lifted him high into the air, the man dangling like a rag doll.

"No." Onkai's voice was like grinding stone, low and filled with malice.

With that, he closed his hand, and the elder's body crumpled with a sickening crunch. Onkai let the corpse fall to the ground, discarded like refuse.

Across the village, more villagers fell. Onkai's presence turned their cries into fuel for his destruction, their despair feeding his strength. He continued to crush homes with ease, the wood snapping like brittle bones under his claws. People were scattered, trampled underfoot, their screams rising to the heavens only to be drowned out by Onkai's guttural laughter.

A young boy cowered in the remains of his family's home, hiding beneath a shattered table. He peeked out, his small body shaking as he saw Onkai tearing through the village. His mother lay nearby, unmoving, and he pressed his hand to his mouth to stifle his sobs. But Onkai could sense the fear in him, the pain that radiated from the boy's tiny body. He turned, his eyes locking on the boy's hiding place.

In one swift motion, Onkai ripped the table away, revealing the terrified child. The boy stared up at him, his eyes wide with horror, his body frozen in fear. Onkai's grin returned, slow and deliberate. He reached down, his massive hand closing around the boy.

The child let out a choked scream as Onkai lifted him into the air, holding him at eye level, singing his delicate skin. Onkai's grip tightened, the boy's bones creaking under the pressure. But before the final crush, Onkai paused. He lowered the boy slightly, letting him dangle helplessly as he whispered, "Run."

The boy, shaking uncontrollably, dropped to the ground the moment Onkai released him. He stumbled backward, eyes wide, before turning and sprinting away into the smoke-filled streets.

Onkai watched him go, the smile never leaving his face. He did not need to kill them all immediately.

Their fear, their hopeless attempts at escape—those were just as sweet as the pain itself.

Just as the boy seemed out of reach, Onkai flicked a single clawed finger, sending a gob of steaming fluid through him.

By the time the fires burned out and the smoke cleared, nothing was left but ruin. The once-peaceful village, a place of healing and harmony, had been reduced to ashes and corpses. Onkai stood at the center of it all, surveying his work, his body radiating power from the pain and suffering he had absorbed.

Satisfied, he turned and walked away, leaving the charred remains of the village in his wake. The earth continued to smolder under his feet, the deep imprints of his steps a permanent scar on the land.

As he disappeared into the mist, the echoes of the few remaining villagers' cries lingered, a haunting reminder of the demon's visit—a legend that would be told in hushed voices for generations to come.

1

WAKAMONO MADE HIS WAY through the market streets of Sanpuku, clutching a list of supplies Red Mist had given him. The city, usually alive with energy, now felt eerily subdued. The crowds were thinner than usual, and the few people who still moved through the market did so in silence, their heads lowered, their movements hurried. It was as though an invisible weight pressed down on the air, heavy and oppressive.

Wakamono noticed it too, the tension. He felt it in the way the wind tugged at his clothes, in the chill that crept along his skin despite the warm afternoon. There was a sense of waiting—like the city itself was holding its breath.

He shifted uncomfortably, his hand instinctively resting on the hilt of his katana, sheathed at his side. It was a habit he had developed since his training with Red Mist had begun. The broken katana, strapped securely in his pack, was his true burden, but the real katana at his hip gave him a sense of readiness. Even so, the unease that had settled over the city was not something a blade could cut through.

The streets were lined with stalls, many of them closed, their tarps pulled tightly over their wares. Those few vendors who remained open glanced around nervously, their hands trembling as they exchanged goods with customers. Conversations were brief, barely more than murmurs. Everyone seemed to be in a hurry to finish their business and retreat to the safety of their homes.

Wakamono wasn't sure when he had first noticed it—the shift in the atmosphere. Maybe it was the way the light seemed duller today, the sun hidden behind a layer of thin clouds that clung stubbornly to the sky. Or maybe it was the way people moved, no longer with purpose but with caution, as if they were expecting something to happen.

His eyes flicked toward a group of townsfolk huddled near the entrance to a side street. They were speaking in hushed tones, their faces pale, eyes darting nervously to the sky and then back to the ground. One of them, a woman wrapped tightly in a fraying shawl, caught his gaze. For a moment, their eyes locked, and Wakamono saw the fear there—raw and unhidden. She quickly turned away, clutching the shawl closer to her body, as if it could shield her from whatever was coming.

Wakamono took a deep breath, feeling the tension settle in his own chest. It was as if the entire city was waiting for something—something bad. He wasn't sure what it was, but his instincts, honed by his training under Red Mist, told him to stay alert.

He approached a vendor selling herbs, handing over a few coins for the supplies Red Mist had requested. The old man behind the stall didn't meet his eyes, his hands shaking slightly as he passed over the small cloth bag. His voice, when he spoke, was low and hurried, as if he wanted Wakamono gone as quickly as possible.

"Dark times," the vendor muttered, his eyes scanning the emptying streets. "Spirits are restless. Evil's at our doorstep..."

Wakamono's grip tightened on his katana. The unease swirling around him was hard to ignore now. He could feel it, thick in the air, like the moments before a storm. He looked toward the sky, noticing for the first time how dark the clouds had grown. They churned above the city, swirling in ominous patterns that didn't belong to a normal weather cycle.

Something was wrong. And the people of Sanpuku weren't the only ones feeling it—Wakamono could sense it too. A faint, creeping chill ran down his spine, and his hand instinctively gripped the hilt of his sword tighter.

He stepped away from the stall, his senses heightened, scanning the square for any sign of danger. The wind picked up again, stirring the dust on the cobblestones. It carried with it the faintest scent of rot—decay that didn't belong in a bustling city like Sanpuku. Wakamono's pulse quickened. His training told him to stay calm, but every instinct he had screamed that something was coming.

And he had a feeling it was about to make itself known.

後見

The wind picked up again, sharper this time, cutting through the market square like a knife. Wakamono tensed, his hand still on the hilt of his katana. He felt the air shift around him, an unnatural gust that made the hair on the back of his neck stand up. His eyes darted around the square, searching for the source of the disturbance.

At first, it was nothing more than a blur, a flicker of motion in the corner of his vision. Then, the wind howled—a high-pitched, eerie screech that seemed to come from everywhere at once. Wakamono turned just in time to see something moving through the air, twisting and darting like a shadow made of wind. It moved too fast to be fully seen, but he caught glimpses: a long, sinuous body with fur that whipped and twisted in the gale, claws sharp as razors glinting in the fading light.

Before he could react, the creature struck. The wind carried it through the square, slashing through the few remaining market patrons with terrifying precision. People screamed, clutching at their arms and legs as thin, red lines appeared across their skin—clean, deep cuts that bled freely. The kamaitachi darted past them, too fast to follow, vanishing into the gusts as quickly as it had appeared.

Wakamono's pulse raced. His heart pounded in his chest as the adrenaline kicked in, sharpening his senses. He had heard of kamaitachi before—spirits of the wind, vicious and deadly, known for attacking without warning and disappearing before anyone could react. But he had never faced one.

His grip tightened on the hilt of his katana. This was it—his first real battle without Red Mist by his side. He had to act.

The wind howled again, and Wakamono spotted the creature's outline racing toward him. Without thinking, he drew his katana in a swift, fluid motion, raising the blade just in time to deflect the first strike. The impact sent a shock through his arms, nearly knocking him off balance, but he held firm. The kamaitachi screeched as it twisted away, vanishing once more into the swirling winds.

Wakamono's eyes darted around the square, searching for the creature. His breath came in quick, shallow bursts, the weight of the moment pressing down on him. He had trained for this—he had practiced every move, every stance—but nothing had prepared him for the speed of a real attack. The kamaitachi was like nothing he had ever faced, its movements too fast to predict, too wild to contain.

The wind shrieked again, and Wakamono spun, swinging his katana in a wide arc. The blade sliced through empty air. He cursed under his breath, frustration mounting. He couldn't see the thing clearly—only flashes of fur, claws, and teeth as it darted in and out of the wind.

Another gust slammed into him from behind, and he barely managed to duck in time as the kamaitachi's claws raked the air where his head had been. He rolled across the cobblestones, coming to his feet in a crouch, his katana held ready. His mind raced—he needed to slow it down, find a way to predict its next move.

The kamaitachi circled him, a faint blur in the air, like a predator stalking its prey. Wakamono's muscles tensed. He could feel the creature watching him, waiting for the perfect moment to strike.

The wind surged again, and this time, Wakamono didn't wait for the attack. He lunged forward, swinging his blade with all the strength he could muster.

The katana sliced through the air, and for a moment, he thought he had it. But the kamaitachi twisted at the last second, avoiding the strike with unnatural speed. Its claws flashed as it retaliated, slashing at Wakamono's arm.

Pain seared through him as the kamaitachi's claws cut deep, but Wakamono gritted his teeth and held his ground. Blood trickled down his arm, but he didn't falter. He had learned from Red Mist that pain was inevitable in battle—what mattered was how he handled it.

He couldn't afford to lose focus now.

The kamaitachi struck again, faster this time. Wakamono parried the first swipe, barely dodged the second, but the third connected, cutting across his leg. He stumbled but kept his footing, refusing to go down. The creature was relentless, but he wasn't giving up.

Then, in a brief moment of clarity, Wakamono remembered something he had read: kamaitachi rode the wind, using it to hide and strike. But they weren't invincible—there was always a pattern to their attacks, a rhythm in the chaos. If he could just find it, he could anticipate its next move.

He took a deep breath, forcing himself to focus, to calm the storm in his own mind. The wind swirled around him, but this time, he didn't let it distract him. He listened—really listened—to the sound of the wind, to the way it moved. There, hidden beneath the howling gusts, was the faintest sound: the flurry of the kamaitachi's claws cutting through the air.

Wakamono turned, his katana raised. The kamaitachi lunged at him, its body a blur of fur and wind. But this time, Wakamono was ready. He swung his katana in a sharp, precise arc, and for the first time, he felt resistance as his blade connected with the creature's body.

The kamaitachi let out a screech of pain, its form flickering as it reeled back. Blood—thick and dark—dripped from its wound, staining the cobblestones.

Wakamono pressed the attack, his movements quicker now, more confident. He swung again, aiming for the same spot, but the kamaitachi was already retreating, its form dissolving into the wind once more.

He staggered, breathing hard, his heart racing. His arm throbbed where the kamaitachi had cut him, but he ignored the pain, scanning the square for any sign of the creature.

The wind was dying down. The kamaitachi was gone.

For now.

Wakamono stood in the middle of the square, chest heaving, blood dripping from his wounds. He had driven it off, but he hadn't defeated it. Not yet. He tightened his grip on the katana, his eyes narrowing as he listened for the faintest sound of its return.

Then, from the shadows at the edge of the square, a figure appeared.

Red Mist.

She moved silently, her eyes calm and calculating as they swept over the scene. She glanced at Wakamono's injuries, then at the blood on the cobblestones where the kamaitachi had retreated. Without a word, she stepped forward, her hand resting on the hilt of her own blade.

"Not bad," she said quietly, her voice steady. "But it's not over yet."

Red Mist stepped past Wakamono, her movements fluid and controlled, as though the chaos of the kamaitachi's attack hadn't fazed her at all. She paused for a moment, scanning the market square, her eyes narrowing as she examined the blood-streaked cobblestones. The air had grown still, but the tension remained thick, as if the wind itself was waiting for another opportunity to strike.

Wakamono wiped the sweat from his brow, breathing hard as he tried to calm his racing heart. His wounds stung, but he forced the pain to the back of his mind. He wasn't sure whether he had driven the kamaitachi off or if it had momentarily retreated, waiting for a better moment to attack again.

"It's fast," he said, his voice low. "I couldn't keep up."

Red Mist glanced at him, her expression unreadable. "You did well," she said, her tone measured. "But remember—speed is not your enemy. Your mind is. Control that, and you can control the battle."

Wakamono nodded, though his frustration was still palpable. He wanted to prove himself, to show that he could handle these threats on his own. But the kamaitachi had been faster than he expected, more dangerous. It was only now, in the quiet after the storm, that he realized just how close he had come to being overwhelmed.

Red Mist turned away from him, her eyes flicking to the shadows that lingered at the edges of the square. "It's not gone," she murmured. "Not completely. Creatures like this... they don't enter civilization on their own accord."

Wakamono frowned, stepping forward to stand beside her. "You mean something brought it here?"

She nodded, her gaze sweeping over the quiet marketplace. "Sanpuku has always had spirits lurking in its corners. But this... this is different. Something's pushing them out of hiding, forcing them into the open."

Before Wakamono could respond, an old man stepped out from the alleyway nearby. He moved with slow, deliberate steps, his shoulders hunched beneath the weight of years. His face was lined with wrinkles, his eyes dull with age, but there was something sharp and knowing about the way he looked at them—like he had seen this all before.

He approached without hesitation, his gaze fixed on Red Mist as though he had expected her to be here.

"Wise to come," the old man rasped, his voice hoarse. "But too late, I fear."

Red Mist regarded him carefully, saying nothing. The old man's gaze flicked briefly to Wakamono, then back to her. He shuffled closer, his breath labored but his words quick, as if time were running out.

"Do you feel it?" he asked, his voice low, conspiratorial. "The darkness... it's moving. Growing."

Wakamono exchanged a glance with Red Mist, unsure of how to respond. The tension in the square was still thick, and the old man's words only added to the unease that clung to the air.

"What are you talking about?" Wakamono asked, stepping forward.

The old man's eyes narrowed, and he raised a shaking finger toward the horizon, where the dark clouds swirled ominously above the city.

"These attacks," he said, his voice barely more than a whisper, "they're not random. The spirits, the creatures—they're being driven out, forced to act. There's something deeper, something darker pushing them." His hand fell to his side, his voice trembling with urgency. "And if the Kōken do not intervene, Sanpuku will fall."

The weight of his words settled over them like a shroud. Wakamono's mind raced, trying to piece together what the old man was saying. Was there truly something bigger, something darker lurking beneath the surface of these attacks?

Red Mist's expression remained unreadable, but Wakamono could see the tension in her posture, the way her hand hovered just above the hilt of her sword. She had sensed it too—the growing threat, the darkness on the horizon.

"We've noticed," Red Mist finally said, her voice calm but firm. "And we will act."

The old man's lips twisted into a grim smile. "Be careful, Kōken. This city's fate rests in your hands."

With that, he turned and shuffled away, disappearing into the shadows as quickly as he had appeared. Wakamono watched him go, the knot of unease in his stomach tightening.

He turned to Red Mist. "Do you believe him?"

She didn't answer right away, her eyes still fixed on the darkening sky. When she finally spoke, her voice was low, thoughtful.

"There's often truth in fear," she said. "We'll find out soon enough."

The wind began to stir again, but this time, it felt different—heavier, like a storm gathering on the horizon. Wakamono stood beside his master as the first droplets of rain began to fall. The unease that had settled over Sanpuku wasn't going anywhere.

It was only beginning.

SANPUKU HAD ALWAYS BEEN a city of life. The markets were the heart of it all, bustling with traders, farmers, and artisans, their wares laid out in colorful displays. Laughter and shouts echoed through the streets, the smell of fresh produce and cooking fires mingling with the crisp mountain air. But now, that vibrant pulse was gone, replaced by a hollow stillness that no one could ignore.

Wakamono moved through the streets, feeling the change in every corner, every shadow. The life that had once filled Sanpuku's veins had drained away, leaving the city cold and tense. The once-lively marketplace was a shadow of its former self. Stalls were half-filled, their owners sitting in silence, casting furtive glances over their shoulders. Conversations, once loud and boisterous, were now murmured whispers, barely more than the hum of fear spreading through the city.

He paused near a vegetable stall, where a vendor sat hunched over, her hands folded tightly in her lap. Her face, once warm and welcoming, was now drawn and pale, her eyes fixed on the ground as though afraid to look up. The vegetables in her baskets, normally lush and vibrant, were wilted, their leaves tinged with brown. A small, shriveled carrot rolled off the edge of the table, but the vendor didn't notice. She stared straight ahead, lost in some private worry, her fingers trembling slightly.

As Wakamono stepped forward to inspect the produce, he overheard bits of conversations from nearby stalls. The voices were low, filled with fear.

"—heard it again last night... the scratching at the walls..."

"—found the livestock dead this morning... eyes wide open, like they saw something..."

"—I'm telling you, I saw it... something moving in the shadows..."

These were not the kinds of stories that belonged in Sanpuku. Not in the city Wakamono had known. But now, they were everywhere. Whispers of strange occurrences, creatures appearing in the dead of night, shadows that didn't belong, and things that no one could explain. The city felt suffocated by fear, the kind that spread silently but quickly, like a fire catching on dry grass.

A gust of wind swept through the marketplace, stirring the dust from the cobblestones. It wasn't a normal breeze. Wakamono could feel it—it carried a chill that didn't match the warm afternoon. The breeze seemed to move through the people, pulling at their clothes, raising the hair on their arms. A collective shudder passed through the crowd as if they could all feel the shift in the air, though no one spoke of it directly.

Wakamono's hand moved to the hilt of his katana, his fingers brushing the cool metal. He didn't draw the blade, but the weight of it at his side was a comfort. He wasn't the only one on edge. The entire city felt like it was holding its breath, waiting for something to happen—something that no one could predict.

He moved farther into the market, his eyes scanning the stalls. More vendors were closing early now, packing their goods with hurried, nervous movements. One man was gathering his produce with such speed that his hands fumbled, spilling a pile of apples onto the ground. He swore under his breath but didn't slow down, glancing up at the sky as though afraid of what might be lurking just out of sight.

A pair of women stood near the well, their heads bent together as they whispered. Wakamono could only catch fragments of their conversation, but it was enough to know they were speaking of the same fears that had gripped the rest of the city.

"...saw it... in my home..."

"...moved by itself... nothing there..."

Their voices were shaky, their faces pale. When one of them glanced over her shoulder, her eyes were wide with a fear that Wakamono had never seen before. She looked around as though expecting something to jump out of the shadows and drag her away.

He kept walking, the knot in his stomach tightening. The fear in Sanpuku was almost tangible now, hanging in the air like a thick fog. Even the animals had begun to sense it. He had seen it himself just days before—a normally docile ox that had snapped its reins and charged through the streets, its eyes wild with terror. The farmers couldn't explain it. They had tried to calm the beast, but it had kicked and bucked, nearly trampling two men before it had finally collapsed from exhaustion.

And it wasn't just the animals. The crops had started to wither too. The farmers spoke in hushed tones of fields that had been full of life one day and dead the next. They said the plants seemed to rot from the inside out, turning black and crumbling to dust in their hands. The market stalls that sold produce were half-empty now, the fruits and vegetables that were still there shriveled and wilted, as though the very land itself had begun to decay.

Wakamono stepped past a stall selling bundles of dried herbs, the vendor's hands trembling as she packed away the last of her goods. She looked up briefly, her eyes meeting Wakamono's, and he saw the same thing he had seen in the faces of everyone he passed—fear. It was etched deep into her features, as though it had taken root inside her, growing stronger every day.

She quickly looked away, her hands moving faster now, stuffing the herbs into her bag. Wakamono lingered for a moment, watching her, but said nothing. There was nothing to say. Whatever was happening in Sanpuku, it was spreading. Fear had wrapped itself around the city like a vice, tightening with every passing hour.

He moved on, his gaze drifting toward the sky. The sun was still high, but the light felt dim, as though a veil had been pulled over it. The clouds were thicker now, darker, swirling above the city in slow, ominous patterns. It was as if the sky itself had changed, reflecting the unease that had settled below.

Wakamono took a deep breath, trying to shake off the feeling, but it clung to him. The tension in the air, the fear in the people's eyes, the strange occurrences that no one could explain—it all pointed to one thing.

Something was coming. Something dark.

And whatever it was, it was already here, hiding in the shadows, waiting.

後見

The sun had started its descent, casting long shadows over Sanpuku. The streets were quieter now, with most of the market stalls closed and people retreating to their homes before nightfall. The air had cooled, but the unease that hung over the city had only deepened.

Wakamono found Red Mist sitting on the low wall that bordered the training yard behind their quarters. She was sharpening her katana, the rhythmic sound of stone against metal echoing in the stillness. Her movements were steady and precise, her face calm, though there was a heaviness in her eyes that hadn't been there before.

Wakamono approached her slowly, his mind still turning over the things he had seen and heard that day. The wilted crops, the animals' strange behavior, the fear in the eyes of the people. It had all been weighing on him, pressing down like an invisible hand on his chest.

Red Mist didn't look up as he approached, but she spoke, her voice low and measured. "You're worried."

It wasn't a question. She knew him too well.

Wakamono stopped a few feet away, his hand resting on the hilt of his katana—a habit. "It's... different," he said, his brow furrowing. "The city. The people. It's like everyone's waiting for something terrible to happen."

Red Mist nodded, still focused on her blade. "They are."

Wakamono swallowed, the knot in his stomach tightening. "I don't understand it. I've seen fear before, but this... it feels like it's everywhere, like the whole city is holding its breath."

For a long moment, Red Mist didn't respond. The soft scraping of the whetstone filled the silence, and Wakamono wondered if she was going to say anything at all. But then she stopped, setting the stone aside and looking up at him.

"You're not wrong," she said quietly. "Something is happening. And it's not just in the city."

Wakamono's pulse quickened. He had suspected as much, but hearing her say it made it real. "What do you think it is?"

Red Mist's gaze drifted toward the horizon, where the last traces of daylight were fading into the clouds. "I don't know," she admitted. "But I've seen things like this before. Fear doesn't spread like this on its own. Something is pushing it. Something is feeding it."

Wakamono felt a chill run down his spine. He had known something was wrong, but to hear Red Mist—a seasoned warrior—acknowledge it so plainly brought the gravity of the situation crashing down on him.

"The creatures people are talking about," he began, trying to piece it together, "the spirits in their homes, the shadows... do you think they're real?"

Red Mist's expression darkened slightly, and she gave a single nod. "They're real."

Wakamono's grip tightened on his sword. "Then why haven't we seen more of them? Why aren't they attacking?"

"They're waiting," Red Mist said simply. "Just like the people are. Something is holding them back for now, but when the time is right, they'll show themselves."

Her words hung in the air, thick and heavy. Wakamono had expected as much, but hearing it confirmed made his chest tighten. He thought of the nightmares, of the shadowy figure that had been haunting him. Was that spirit waiting too? Was it watching him, just as the others were watching the city?

"I don't like this," Wakamono muttered, shaking his head. "I can't stand just sitting here, waiting for something to happen."

Red Mist stood, sliding her katana into its sheath with a soft click. She stepped closer, her presence steady and commanding, but there was a softness in her eyes as she looked at him.

"Patience is part of the battle," she said. "Sometimes the hardest fight is the one where you don't draw your sword."

Wakamono frowned, his frustration bubbling to the surface. "But what if we're not ready? What if they're too strong when they finally come?"

Red Mist studied him for a moment, her gaze steady. "That's why we don't sit idle. We prepare.

We sharpen our skills and our minds along with our weapons. And when the time comes, we'll be ready."

Wakamono let out a breath he hadn't realized he'd been holding. Her words made sense, but they didn't make the tension any easier to bear. He nodded, though the unease in his chest remained.

Red Mist placed a hand on his shoulder, her grip firm but reassuring. "Trust your training. And trust yourself. Fear is a weapon we don't let our enemies use against us."

Wakamono met her gaze, seeing the strength in her eyes. She believed in him—believed in both of them. And for a moment, it eased the weight that had been pressing down on him all day.

"Now," she said, stepping back and nodding toward the training yard, "show me what you've learned. The spirits aren't the only ones preparing for what's to come."

Wakamono smiled faintly, drawing his sword as he followed her into the yard. The unease still lingered, but at least now, it felt like there was something he could do about it.

後見

The fog was thick—so thick that Wakamono couldn't see more than a few feet in front of him. He moved through it slowly, his footsteps muffled by the heavy silence that pressed in on all sides. The air was cold, unnaturally so, and with every breath he took, his lungs seemed to fill with frost. He couldn't see where he was going, but it didn't matter. In this dream, he never knew where he was. The only thing he knew was that something was watching him.

He could feel it.

The fog shifted, swirling around him in slow, deliberate patterns. Shadows flickered at the edge of his vision—dark shapes that moved just out of reach, too quick to catch but too slow to ignore. They were everywhere, slipping between the tendrils of mist, their forms twisting and bending in unnatural ways.

Wakamono strained to see them, his eyes scanning the fog, but the shadows never stayed still long enough for him to focus. They were like smoke, slipping through his fingers the moment he tried to grasp them. One moment, they were large, hulking figures that towered over him, their outlines jagged and monstrous. The next, they were small and fast, darting through the mist like wolves on the hunt. Always moving, always just out of sight.

He kept walking, his heartbeat quickening. His hand went to his side, where his katana should have been, but in this place, he was unarmed. He was always unarmed here, vulnerable. The shadows knew it. They thrived on it.

The silence deepened, the air thick with anticipation. Wakamono's breath came in shallow bursts, each step feeling heavier than the last. The fog seemed to pull at him, slowing his movements, dragging him deeper into the unknown. He didn't know where he was going, but there was no turning back. He had to keep moving. He had to get away.

But away from what?

He glanced over his shoulder, his pulse pounding in his ears. The shadows followed him, silent and relentless. They were closer now—he could feel their presence pressing in, watching him. The hair on the back of his neck stood on end, a chill running down his spine. He quickened his pace, his feet moving faster, but no matter how fast he went, the shadows kept pace with him, their forms shifting and swirling in the mist.

A low sound rumbled in the distance, like the growl of some unseen beast. Wakamono froze, his heart hammering in his chest. The fog seemed to thicken, closing in around him. The growl came again, louder this time, vibrating through the ground beneath his feet. He turned slowly, his eyes straining to see through the thick veil of mist.

That's when he saw it.

A figure—a hulking, monstrous silhouette—stood at the edge of the fog. It was massive, far larger than anything Wakamono had ever faced, its form hidden in the swirling gray. It didn't move. It didn't need to. Its very presence was enough to send a wave of cold fear through Wakamono's body.

The figure had no face that he could see, no features he could make out. But its eyes… its eyes burned through the mist, two glowing orbs of fiery red that cut through the fog like blades. They watched him, unblinking, unwavering. Wakamono couldn't move. He couldn't breathe.

The ground shifted beneath his feet, the fog swirling violently around him as the figure took a single step forward. The growl rumbled again, deep and resonant, like the earth itself was trembling in fear. The shadows in the mist twisted, writhing as if pulled toward the figure, drawn to its dark energy.

Wakamono's legs felt like stone, rooted to the spot. His heart raced, every instinct screaming at him to run, but his body refused to move. The figure stepped closer, its massive form barely visible through the swirling fog, but those eyes—those burning, hateful eyes—never left him.

A cold wind whipped through the mist, carrying with it the faintest whisper, a voice so low it barely reached his ears.

"I see you…"

The voice wasn't human. It was dark, twisted, filled with malice and hunger. It was a voice that belonged to the shadows, to the thing that watched him from the depths of his nightmares.

The figure moved again, another step closer. Wakamono felt the air shift around him, felt the weight of its gaze pressing down on him like a vice. His breath came in short, panicked gasps, his throat tight, his chest heavy. He wanted to scream, to shout, but no sound came. The figure was too close now, its eyes burning through him, piercing his soul.

"I see you..."

The words echoed in his mind, louder now, relentless. The fog swirled faster, the shadows closing in, tightening around him like a trap. Wakamono's body trembled, his legs finally moving as he stumbled backward, desperate to escape. But there was nowhere to go.

The figure loomed over him now, its massive form towering in the mist. The air crackled with tension, and the ground beneath him seemed to tremble. The eyes blazed brighter, filling his vision with burning red light, consuming everything.

And then, just as the darkness seemed ready to swallow him whole—

三

WAKAMONO'S EYES SNAPPED OPEN, the remnants of his latest nightmare still clinging to him like the mist in his dreams. His body was tense, his skin damp with sweat, and his heart thudded against his chest. For a long moment, he lay still, staring at the ceiling, trying to calm the racing thoughts in his mind. But no matter how hard he tried, the dream wouldn't leave him. It never did.

The shadowy figure—the one with the burning eyes—had been closer this time. He could still feel its gaze, as if it had followed him out of the dream and into the waking world. His skin prickled at the thought, and a chill ran down his spine.

With a soft sigh, Wakamono sat up, rubbing his hands over his face. His body ached from the restless night, and his mind felt sluggish, weighed down by the lingering fear. He couldn't stay here. Not in this room, not with the feeling of those eyes still pressing down on him.

He needed air. He needed to get away from the oppressive atmosphere of the city, even if just for a little while.

Wakamono dressed quickly, the familiar weight of his katana settling at his side as he strapped it on. His fingers brushed the hilt, a small comfort in the midst of his unease. Without a sound, he slipped out of the room and made his way through the quiet halls of their quarters. The early morning light barely filtered through the windows, casting long shadows along the walls.

He stepped outside into the cool morning air, hoping that the fresh breeze might clear his mind. But the moment his feet touched the cobblestone streets, he felt it again—that heavy, suffocating tension that seemed to hang over Sanpuku like a cloud.

The city was still waking up, the streets nearly empty. A few vendors were setting up their stalls in the marketplace, but even they moved with a slowness that spoke of the same unease that gripped Wakamono. The tension was everywhere now, in the way people walked, in the way they spoke, in the way the air itself seemed thicker, heavier.

Wakamono pulled his cloak tighter around his shoulders and headed toward the outskirts of the city, his mind set on finding some space to breathe, to escape the weight that pressed down on him. As he walked, the sounds of the city faded behind him, replaced by the soft rustle of leaves and the distant calls of birds waking to the day. The familiar sights of Sanpuku's outer streets, with their winding paths and small clusters of trees, should have brought him some comfort, but today they felt different.

No matter how far he walked, the sensation followed him—the feeling of being watched, of something lurking just beyond his sight. It had been there in his dreams, and now it clung to him like a shadow.

Wakamono's hand rested on the hilt of his katana, his fingers tightening around the grip. He knew it was just the lingering effects of the nightmare, but the fear felt real enough. His eyes darted around, scanning the empty streets and the trees that lined the path, but there was nothing. No movement, no sound out of place. Just the soft whisper of the wind through the leaves.

And yet... the feeling wouldn't leave him.

He kept walking, his footsteps slow and deliberate, his mind racing. He tried to shake it off, to focus on the normalcy of his surroundings. The city's edge had always been a place of peace for him—a place where he could clear his mind after long days of training. But now, even this place felt tainted by the darkness that had settled over Sanpuku.

The dream was still with him, haunting him even now. The shadowy figure, those burning eyes—he couldn't get them out of his head. Every time he closed his eyes, he saw them. Every time the wind shifted, he half-expected to hear the low growl that had echoed through the fog in his dreams.

Wakamono shook his head, trying to clear the thoughts from his mind. He had to focus. He couldn't let the dream control him, couldn't let it seep into his waking hours. He was better than that. Red Mist had trained him to be better than that.

But no matter how hard he tried to push the fear away, it clung to him. The weight of it pressed down on his chest, tightening with every step.

He was almost at the edge of the city now. The path wound through a small grove of trees, their branches swaying gently in the breeze. Normally, the sound would have soothed him, but today, it only heightened his sense of unease. Every creak of a branch, every rustle of leaves, seemed to carry with it the promise of something darker, something hiding just out of sight.

Wakamono slowed his pace, his eyes narrowing as he scanned the trees. The shadows beneath the branches seemed deeper than usual, darker. He couldn't shake the feeling that something was watching him from within those shadows. Were these Kōken instincts, or the fears of a young man?

He paused at the edge of the grove, listening. The city was behind him now, its sounds faint in the distance. Ahead, there was nothing but the soft rustle of leaves and the distant calls of birds.

But the feeling wouldn't leave him. That weight, that pressure—it was still there, growing heavier with every passing moment.

He took a deep breath, trying to calm his racing heart. It was just the dream. Just the lingering effects of a restless night. There was nothing here. Nothing to be afraid of.

And yet, as he stood there, staring into the shadows beneath the trees, Wakamono couldn't help but feel that he wasn't alone.

Wakamono's thoughts kept circling back to the dream as he walked, the shadowy figure with burning eyes looming large in his mind. The chill of the air, the heavy atmosphere—none of it felt right, even now that he was awake. The old seer's words echoed in his thoughts. *"The brighter you burn, the longer the shadows become."*

What would the old man have made of his nightmares? Of the figure that seemed so real, so present? Would he have said the spirits were growing restless, drawn by the rising darkness? Wakamono tried to push the thoughts away, but the unease clung to him. He needed to clear his mind, focus on the real world around him.

But as he walked, something shifted.

Without warning, Wakamono stopped short, confusion knitting his brow. The path in front of him seemed to change in an instant. A wall—a force, invisible but solid—rose out of nowhere, blocking his way. He reached out cautiously, his fingers brushing against something cold and unyielding. It wasn't stone or wood, but something that felt like resistance itself. There was nothing visible in front of him, yet the barrier was unmistakable.

His heart thudded in his chest, a chill creeping up his spine. He stepped to the side, trying to go around it, but the wall moved with him, shifting silently to block his way again. Wakamono's pulse quickened, his breath shallow as he turned, testing the limits of the invisible trap. No matter which way he moved, the wall was there—pressing in, unyielding.

"An illusion…" he muttered, his voice tinged with uncertainty. "It has to be."

But when he tried to step back, he found the same barrier behind him. Panic bubbled at the edges of his mind, the space around him shrinking, the air growing thinner. The wall wasn't physical, but it felt real enough—closing in, tightening around him like a cage.

His instincts kicked in, and his hand shot to the hilt of his katana. He drew the blade in one swift motion and slashed at the air in front of him. The blade cut through the space where the wall should have been, but it made no difference. The barrier remained, growing heavier, more suffocating.

His breath came faster, and for a moment, the shadows from his dream seemed to blur with reality. His body tensed, every muscle screaming at him to fight, to break free. But no matter how hard he swung, the invisible wall wouldn't yield. His strikes felt pointless, his efforts swallowed by the empty air.

Panic surged in his chest, his thoughts scattering. The walls—were they closing in? The air was growing colder, thinner. He could barely breathe. His heartbeat pounded in his ears, and his vision narrowed, the world shrinking to the space of the invisible prison around him.

Wakamono stumbled back, his pulse racing. He felt the pressure of the walls closing in around him, his mind teetering on the edge of full panic. He couldn't fight this. His katana was useless here. The walls were tightening, his breath coming in short, sharp gasps.

Then something clicked.

His eyes darted around the space, his thoughts racing. *This isn't real,* he told himself, the words coming slow at first, but growing louder in his mind. *It's a trick. The nurikabe isn't real.* He remembered the stories—how the nurikabe fed on confusion, on fear. It wasn't a physical thing. It was a barrier of the mind, invading his thoughts.

He closed his eyes, forcing himself to take a slow, steady breath. His heart still raced, his muscles tense, but he knew now that fighting wasn't the answer. This wasn't something he could break with a blade.

Wakamono focused, drawing in another slow breath, pushing down the panic that swirled in his chest. The weight of the invisible walls pressed against him, but he held his ground, refusing to give in to the fear. He let the katana fall to his side, his grip loosening as he took another breath, this one deeper, steadier.

He opened his eyes and focused on the path ahead. The wall was still there, invisible but present, a looming pressure against his mind. But now, Wakamono understood. The nurikabe wasn't real—it was only there as long as he believed it was.

Calm, he told himself. *Focus.*

With slow, deliberate steps, he moved forward. At first, the barrier resisted, pressing against him, heavy and unyielding. But Wakamono didn't stop. He kept moving, one step at a time, his breath steady, his mind focused. The pressure pushed against him, but he didn't let it shake him. He walked through it, his will stronger than the illusion.

And then, just like that, the weight lifted.

The cold air thinned, the walls vanished, and the path ahead was clear. Wakamono exhaled slowly, his body still tense, but the sense of relief was palpable. The nurikabe was gone. He had broken through it—not with his sword, but with his mind.

He stood there for a moment, catching his breath. The shadows that had clung to him moments before seemed to fade, leaving only the quiet of the path ahead.

For the first time in what felt like hours, Wakamono felt a flicker of confidence. He had gotten himself out of the trap. He was learning.

But even as the weight of the nurikabe faded, the sense of something watching him—something much darker—remained.

後見

Wakamono made his way deeper into the wilderness, following a familiar path through the trees. It was a route he had walked many times before, leading to a small clearing nestled between the hills, where the trees opened up to reveal a tranquil spot surrounded by tall grass and wildflowers. This place had become his own over the years—a retreat, a sanctuary where he could find calm amidst the chaos of his training and the growing tension in the city.

As he neared the clearing, a sense of relief began to wash over him. The air here was different, cleaner, untouched by the fear that clung to Sanpuku. The trees were tall and strong, their branches swaying gently in the breeze, casting dappled shadows on the forest floor. Birds flitted between the branches, their soft calls soothing in the quiet of the morning.

Wakamono stepped into the clearing, feeling the tension in his body begin to ease. The place was as it had always been—peaceful, untouched. He walked to the center and sat down on the soft grass, crossing his legs and resting his hands on his knees. His katana lay by his side, but here, he didn't feel the need to keep his hand on the hilt.

He closed his eyes and took a deep breath, letting the fresh air fill his lungs. Slowly, he exhaled, focusing on the rhythm of his breathing. In. Out. The sounds of the wilderness surrounded him—the rustling of leaves, the distant chirping of birds, the soft murmur of the wind through the trees.

For a few moments, the weight of his recent encounters—the dreams, the shadows, the nurik-abe—began to fade. This place had always brought him peace, and he sank deeper into that calm, his mind settling into a state of quiet meditation.

But then... something shifted.

At first, it was subtle. The sounds of the forest seemed to grow distant, the wind slowing, the birdsong fading to silence. The air, once fresh and cool, became heavy, oppressive. Wakamono's breath hitched in his throat, his heartbeat quickening. He tried to focus, to steady himself, but the calm he had been reaching for was slipping away.

Then, in the darkness behind his closed eyes, he saw it—a flicker of light, faint at first, like the glow of embers. He ignored it, trying to pull himself back into his meditation, but the light grew stronger, burning brighter until it was impossible to ignore.

Wakamono's eyes snapped open, but the scene before him wasn't the peaceful clearing he had come to know.

It was gone.

The tall trees were nothing but blackened, twisted husks, their branches stripped bare and reaching like claws toward a sky choked with smoke. The soft grass beneath him was scorched and cracked, the earth split and broken, as though the very ground had been torn apart by some unimaginable force.

Flames licked at the edges of the clearing, creeping closer, their heat searing his skin. The air was thick with ash, the acrid smell of burning wood and earth filling his lungs, choking him. The once-vibrant place of peace was now a wasteland, consumed by fire and destruction.

And there, in the center of it all, he saw himself.

Wakamono stared, frozen, as the vision of his own form sat where he had just been, in the same meditative pose, eyes closed. But this version of himself was surrounded by flames, the fire creeping closer, licking at his clothes, his skin. The earth beneath him crumbled, splitting wide, the ground falling away into darkness.

He tried to move, to scream, but his body wouldn't obey. He was rooted to the spot, watching as the vision of himself sat in silence, oblivious to the destruction that surrounded him.

Then, in the distance, a familiar sound—low, rumbling, like the growl of some unseen beast.

Wakamono's breath caught in his throat. He knew what was coming. He had heard it before.

The shadows shifted, twisting through the flames, and there, just beyond the edge of the burning clearing, he saw them—two burning red eyes.

They glowed in the darkness, piercing through the smoke and fire, watching him, unblinking. The same eyes that had haunted his dreams, the same eyes that had followed him, always watching.

I see you...

The voice was low, distorted, like a whisper carried on the wind. It echoed in his mind, repeating over and over, each word heavier, more oppressive.

I see you...

The flames grew higher, consuming the vision of himself, the fire swallowing everything. The trees collapsed in on themselves, the earth split wide, and the sky itself seemed to shatter as the fire roared around him.

Wakamono's heart pounded in his chest, his breath coming in ragged gasps. The heat was unbearable, the pressure of the burning gaze pressing down on him, crushing him.

I see you...

The words were everywhere, all around him, inside him. He tried to move, tried to break free, but the flames held him in place, the red eyes locked on him, watching, always watching.

I see you...

Wakamono jolted awake, gasping for breath. His heart raced, his skin slick with sweat, and for a moment, he was disoriented, his mind still reeling from the vision. But when his eyes focused, he found himself back in the clearing.

The trees were tall and green. The grass was soft beneath him, untouched by flames. The birds had returned, their soft calls filling the air once more. Everything was as it had been before.

But the image of destruction lingered in his mind—the blackened earth, the burning trees, and those eyes... always watching.

He sat there, his chest rising and falling with each labored breath, his mind racing.

後見

Wakamono returned to the quarters he shared with Red Mist, his body still tense, his thoughts spinning. He needed answers. And there was only one person he trusted enough to share what he had seen.

Red Mist was standing by the window, her katana resting against the wall as she gazed out at the city. Even from a distance, Wakamono could see the furrow in her brow—the same tension that seemed to be spreading throughout Sanpuku. She turned slightly as he entered the room, her sharp eyes catching the unease written across his face.

"Something happened," she said, her voice calm but probing.

Wakamono nodded, crossing the room in a few quick strides. He felt the weight of his katana at his side, but it did little to comfort him now.

"I had another vision," he said, his voice quiet. "But this time it wasn't just a dream."

Red Mist's gaze sharpened, her full attention now on him. "What did you see?"

Wakamono hesitated, unsure how to explain the intensity of the vision, the way the peaceful clearing had turned into a nightmare. But he forced the words out, describing the burning trees, the cracked earth, the flames surrounding him, and—most of all—the red eyes.

"They were there again," he said, his voice tightening. "The same eyes that I've been seeing in my dreams. And I heard it again too... *'I see you.'* It was like... it was speaking directly to me."

Red Mist remained silent for a moment, her expression unreadable. Then she turned away from the window, her movements slow and deliberate.

"That's not just a dream, Wakamono," she said quietly. "It's something more."

Wakamono swallowed, his pulse quickening. He had feared as much, but hearing Red Mist confirm it made the reality of the situation feel heavier. "What do we do?" he asked, his voice strained. "We need answers. Maybe Kaida—"

Red Mist cut him off with a shake of her head. "We can't go to Kaida. Not now."

"But Kaida knows about spirits, about visions," Wakamono protested. "He might be able to help us understand what's happening."

"I know," Red Mist said, her tone firm but not unkind. "But the city is on edge. Spirits and beasts are appearing everywhere, and people are afraid. Leaving Sanpuku now would be reckless."

Wakamono's shoulders slumped. He knew she was right. The city was in a fragile state, and any absence—especially hers—could make things worse.

Still, the frustration gnawed at him. He wanted to do something, anything, to find out what was haunting him.

"What do we do, then?" he asked again, his voice quieter this time.

Red Mist paused, considering the question. Then she looked at him, her expression softening slightly. "We'll split up."

Wakamono blinked. "Split up?"

"You're right—we need answers," she said. "But we also need to stay close to the city. I'll investigate some of the areas around Sanpuku where spirit and beast incidents have been the most frequent. In the meantime, you can start going through the scrolls."

Wakamono frowned. "Scrolls?"

Red Mist nodded. "There are ancient texts in the archives—scrolls that speak of spirits and demons. You might find something that points to the creature in your visions."

Wakamono hesitated, the idea of combing through dusty old texts less appealing than the thought of going out into the field with her. But he knew that Red Mist was right. His visions were tied to something ancient, something that might have been documented long ago.

"All right," he said after a moment. "I'll look through the scrolls."

Red Mist gave a small nod, her eyes searching his face. "Be thorough. And keep your mind open—sometimes the answers aren't obvious."

Wakamono nodded.

"I'll head to the outskirts," Red Mist continued. "There have been reports of spirits gathering near the old shrines. I'll see if there's anything we've missed."

Wakamono's pulse quickened at the thought of her going out alone, but he didn't voice his concern. Red Mist had been doing this long before he came into her life. She didn't need his worry.

"Be careful," he said, his voice low.

With that, Red Mist turned, gathering her belongings with the practiced efficiency of someone who had spent a lifetime on the move. Within moments, she was gone, the door closing softly behind her.

Wakamono stood there for a long moment, staring at the empty space where she had been. His mind was still buzzing with questions, his body thrumming with the need for action. But he had his orders. And if there was one thing Red Mist had taught him, it was that there was always a way to find answers—if you knew where to look.

With a sigh, Wakamono turned toward the archives, where the ancient scrolls awaited him. He would find answers. He had to.

四

THE SCENT OF DUST and age filled Wakamono's nostrils as he stepped into the dimly lit archives. The room was cool, the air heavy with the weight of centuries of knowledge stored away in ancient scrolls and brittle tomes. It was a place of silence, where the past was carefully kept, though often forgotten by the outside world. Wakamono had been here before, though not often—Red Mist had typically been the one to consult the ancient texts when they needed guidance.

But now, he was on his own.

Rows of shelves lined the walls, stacked high with scrolls that ranged from well-worn and faded to completely untouched. Some looked as though they might crumble at the slightest touch, their edges curled and yellowed with age. Others were bound with delicate cords, seals still intact, as if no one had dared to open them in decades, maybe centuries.

Wakamono's footsteps echoed softly in the stillness as he approached the nearest shelf. His eyes scanned the spines of the scrolls, searching for something—anything—that might point him in the right direction. He wasn't even sure what he was looking for, only that it had to be here, buried somewhere in the midst of these musty old records.

He reached out and gingerly took hold of one of the scrolls, the parchment feeling rough and dry beneath his fingers. He unrolled it slowly, careful not to damage it. The script inside was faded, almost illegible in places, but Wakamono could make out fragments of ancient tales—stories of spirits, demons, and long-forgotten battles. But none of it was useful.

Wakamono sighed, rolling the scroll back up and placing it carefully on the shelf. He moved to the next one, repeating the process. Scroll after scroll, each one filled with old stories and records, but none of them contained what he needed.

As the hours passed, his frustration grew.

The more he searched, the more futile it felt. These scrolls were too old, too distant from the present threat. They spoke of creatures he had never heard of—spirits bound to mountains long lost, demons that had been vanquished centuries ago. Every scroll he picked up seemed to drift further from the answers he sought, and the dust clung to his hands, reminding him just how long these records had been buried away, untouched.

He could hear the quiet creak of the wooden shelves as he moved between them, the silence only amplifying his growing impatience. His mind kept wandering back to Red Mist—out there in the field, confronting the spirits and beasts directly. She was hunting for answers, doing something tangible, while he was stuck here, sifting through papers that crumbled at his touch.

Wakamono unrolled another scroll, the corners of the parchment flaking off as he carefully flattened it out. His brow furrowed as he tried to make sense of the faded script, but the symbols were so ancient they barely resembled the language he knew. He squinted, trying to decipher the strange shapes, but his patience was wearing thin.

He slammed the scroll down, the motion more forceful than he intended. The fragile parchment crackled beneath his fingers, and he winced, cursing under his breath as he set it aside. His hands were coated in dust, his head aching from hours of reading words that led nowhere.

"This is pointless," he muttered to himself, rubbing his temples in frustration.

The walls of the archive seemed to press in on him, the air thick with age and disuse. He could feel the weight of the silence, the stillness suffocating him. While Red Mist was out there, facing danger head-on, he was stuck here, lost in a sea of forgotten knowledge.

Wakamono stood and paced for a moment, the quiet of the archive doing little to calm his restless energy. He wanted to be out there—fighting, searching, confronting whatever was out there. But instead, he was here, with nothing to show for his efforts.

After a few deep breaths, he forced himself to sit back down and continue the search. There had to be something here. There had to be.

Wakamono moved to another shelf, his eyes scanning the rows of scrolls, each one looking older and more fragile than the last. His fingers hovered over one particularly ancient scroll, nearly disintegrated with age. The edges were frayed, the once-vibrant ink now a faded gray, almost indistinguishable from the parchment.

Something about this scroll caught his attention.

Carefully, he reached for it, his fingers trembling slightly as he lifted it from its resting place. The scroll was light, as if time had drained it of its weight, leaving only a fragile shell behind. Wakamono unrolled it slowly, the parchment almost crumbling in his hands.

The script inside was unlike anything he had seen before. The symbols were strange, foreign, as though they belonged to a language long forgotten. They spiraled across the page in intricate patterns, weaving together in a way that seemed more like a spell than a story.

Wakamono's breath caught in his throat as he scanned the strange script. He couldn't read it, not exactly, but there was something about it—something that made his pulse quicken, that whispered of hidden secrets and ancient power.

This scroll... it was different.

Wakamono leaned in closer, his eyes tracing the unfamiliar symbols. He couldn't make sense of them, but he could feel the significance behind them, as though the scroll itself held a key to something much larger than the other dusty texts that surrounded him.

For the first time that day, a flicker of hope stirred in Wakamono's chest. Maybe—just maybe—this scroll held the answers he was searching for.

Wakamono's eyes narrowed as he carefully scanned the ancient symbols on the scroll, trying to make sense of the strange script. It was unlike any language he had encountered before, its markings intricate and winding, as if each symbol held layers of meaning hidden beneath the surface. The parchment was so fragile that he barely dared to touch it, and yet, something about the scroll felt important—urgent, even.

His fingers traced a few of the symbols, searching for anything familiar, any clue that might connect this scroll to the vision of the red-eyed monstrosity that haunted him. At first, it seemed hopeless—just another indecipherable relic of the past. But as he studied the patterns more closely, a few phrases began to take shape, faint echoes of an ancient language buried deep in his training.

The symbols for *watching* and *burning* seemed to repeat themselves, woven throughout the script like a hidden warning. And there—near the center—was a symbol he couldn't ignore. It was a pair of eyes, drawn in thick, deliberate strokes, and it was unmistakably familiar. The same fiery red eyes he had seen in his visions. The same eyes that had been watching him.

Wakamono's breath caught in his throat. The scroll was talking about it—about the creature. He was sure of it.

His heart raced as he tried to decipher more, but the symbols became more complex the further he read. His knowledge was limited, and the ancient script was too fragmented for him to fully understand. Frustration bubbled up inside him. The answers were right in front of him, just out of reach, hidden behind the layers of time and language.

He needed help.

Wakamono rolled the scroll back up with careful hands, his mind still buzzing with half-formed thoughts. He would need someone who understood these symbols, someone who could read the language of the past. The clerk at the archive might know where to find such a person.

The clerk was a thin, bespectacled man, hunched over a desk covered in papers and ink-stained quills. He looked up as Wakamono approached, blinking slowly as though he hadn't had much company in recent days.

"Can I help you?" the clerk asked, his voice dry and tired.

Wakamono held up the scroll, trying to keep his impatience in check. "I found this in the archives. It's… important. I need someone who can read the script. Do you know anyone?"

The clerk squinted at the scroll but didn't reach for it. "I'm not much for ancient languages, I'm afraid," he said, tapping his fingers idly on the desk. "But there is someone. An old historian, lives in the northern district. Specializes in things like this."

Wakamono felt a flicker of hope. "What's their name?"

"Her name's Shiki," the clerk replied, scratching his head as though trying to remember more. "Very old. Very eccentric. But if anyone can make sense of that scroll, it's her."

"Where can I find her?"

The clerk gave Wakamono directions, though it was clear he didn't expect the young Kōken to have much luck with Shiki. "She's… particular," the clerk added. "Likes things done a certain way. Doesn't take well to people rushing her."

Wakamono gritted his teeth but nodded. He wasn't in the mood for quirks or habits, but he needed answers. And if Shiki was the one who could give them to him, he would find her.

後見

The northern district of Sanpuku was far quieter than the rest of the city, a place where the streets narrowed and twisted, and the buildings leaned inward as though they were conspiring in whispered secrets. The houses here were older, their wooden frames weathered by time and neglect. Ivy crawled up the walls of many, and the windows seemed to hold an eternal layer of dust, clouding any view from the outside.

Wakamono followed the directions the clerk had given him, finally arriving at a small, unassuming house wedged between two larger, more imposing buildings. The house was practically swallowed by the ivy clinging to its walls, and the roof sagged slightly under the weight of years. There was an odd sense of stillness about the place, as though time itself had slowed the moment he stepped onto the narrow path leading to the front door.

He knocked firmly but heard no response. After a moment, he knocked again, louder this time.

At last, the door creaked open, but only by a sliver, just wide enough for a single eye to peer out at him from the darkness beyond.

"Yes?" came a voice, sharp and thin, like a thread pulled tight.

Wakamono held up the scroll in response, his tone measured. "I'm looking for Shiki. I was told she could help me with this."

The eye narrowed suspiciously, and there was a long pause. Then, with a soft sigh, the door creaked open just a bit more, revealing a hunched woman draped in layers of worn robes. Her frame was slight but held a strange elegance. Her gray hair hung in loose, wispy strands around her face, and her eyes were sharp, gleaming with an intelligence that belied her age. Deep lines creased her face, carved by the weight of years, but her movements were careful, deliberate, as though every step and gesture was part of some private ritual.

She looked Wakamono up and down, her eyes lingering on the scroll before drifting back to his face. "Young one, aren't you?" she muttered, more to herself than to him. Her voice was raspy, like dried leaves brushing together, but there was an odd warmth beneath the words.

"Come in," she said, shuffling back into the house without waiting for a reply. "But don't touch anything."

Wakamono stepped inside cautiously, his eyes adjusting to the dim light. The air was thick with the smell of incense, herbs, and something else—something older, mustier, like the scent of old books left untouched for centuries. The walls were lined with shelves, each one packed with jars, scrolls, and strange trinkets that seemed to serve no clear purpose. Some were covered in dust, while others appeared to have been placed with meticulous care.

A small table sat in the center of the room, surrounded by cushions that had long since lost their shape. Every corner of the house seemed filled with objects of varying degrees of mystery—vials filled with liquid, brittle feathers tied together with string, dried plants hanging from the ceiling beams, and ancient artifacts whose origins Wakamono couldn't begin to guess.

Shiki moved with surprising grace despite her hunched posture, but her steps were slow, as though she was following an invisible map of where each foot must fall. She moved toward a low table in the center of the room and gestured for Wakamono to sit.

Wakamono did as instructed, lowering himself onto one of the worn cushions. He couldn't help but feel out of place in this cluttered, ritualistic environment. His mind was racing, eager to unravel the mystery of the scroll, but here, everything seemed to move at its own pace—a pace far slower than he could tolerate.

"Tea?" Shiki asked, her back still turned to him as she began lighting a stick of incense. She didn't wait for his answer before retrieving a small teapot from a shelf.

"No, thank you," Wakamono replied, though his voice carried an edge of impatience that he tried to suppress.

Shiki, however, appeared entirely unaffected by his tone. She moved with painstaking care, lighting the incense, adjusting the position of a small brass figurine, and finally setting the teapot on the low stove in the corner. Her movements were slow, precise, as though everything had to be in its exact place before she could focus on anything else.

Wakamono watched her, trying to keep his frustration in check. His fingers drummed lightly against his knee, but he quickly stopped, sensing that even the slightest fidgeting might disrupt the delicate order of this room. He knew better than to rush someone like Shiki, but every second felt like an eternity. Red Mist was out there, facing danger and hunting for answers, while he was stuck here, waiting for a woman who moved at the speed of molasses.

Finally, after what felt like an excruciatingly long pause, Shiki sat down across from him, folding her hands neatly in her lap. She glanced at the incense she had lit, nodding slightly as if satisfied with the balance of the room. Only then did she turn her sharp eyes back to Wakamono.

"You've come to ask about something you don't understand," she said, her voice carrying an air of amusement. "Most people do."

Wakamono forced a polite smile, though inwardly, he was anything but amused. "It's this scroll," he said, holding it up. "I found it in the archives. The symbols—they seem to describe something I've been seeing in my visions. Something dangerous."

Shiki's eyes flickered with curiosity, but she didn't reach for the scroll right away. Instead, she leaned back slightly, studying Wakamono as if he were a puzzle she needed to solve. "Dangerous, is it?" she mused. "Danger is a relative thing, young Kōken. What is dangerous to one may be quite ordinary to another."

Wakamono clenched his jaw, forcing himself to remain calm. "This isn't ordinary," he said, his voice steady but firm. "It's a creature. I've seen it in my dreams—red eyes, burning. It's watching me. I think this scroll might help me understand it."

Shiki's lips curved into a small, knowing smile, but she didn't rush. She motioned to the empty tea cups with her eyes. Wakamono poured her some tea. Shiki appeared to drink with deliberate slowness, taking a long, careful sip before placing the cup back down. "Visions are tricky things, young one," she said, her tone light, as though they were discussing the weather. "Sometimes they show us the truth. Sometimes they show us what we fear."

Wakamono couldn't hide his impatience any longer. "I don't have time for riddles. Please, I need to know what this means."

For a moment, the room fell into a deep silence, broken only by the faint crackle of the incense burning nearby. Shiki looked at him, her expression unreadable, but the weight of her gaze was clear. She wasn't one to be rushed, no matter how urgent the situation felt to him.

"Young people," she said softly, more to herself than to him. "Always in such a hurry."

Finally, with a slow, deliberate movement, she extended a hand. "Let me see this scroll you're so concerned about."

Wakamono handed it over, his pulse quickening as she unrolled the fragile parchment. Shiki's eyes, sharp despite her age, flicked over the symbols with a practiced ease. For a long time, she said nothing, simply studying the text, her face betraying no emotion.

Wakamono could barely stand the silence. "Well?" he asked, unable to keep the edge from his voice.

Shiki glanced up at him, a slow smile creeping across her face. "Ah... yes. I can see why you've come to me." She rolled the scroll back up carefully, placing it on the table in front of her. "But this will take time, young one. Time, and perhaps more patience than you're used to."

Wakamono opened his mouth to protest, but she raised a hand, silencing him with a look that brokered no argument.

"I'll take a look," she said, her tone final. "Come back tomorrow. Maybe I'll have something for you then."

THE ROAD LEADING OUT of Sanpuku was narrow, winding through the foothills in a path that seemed to grow more uneven with every step. Red Mist moved swiftly, her eyes scanning the landscape as she followed the path, her katana at her side. The air here felt different—heavier, as if the land itself was holding its breath. The clouds hung low in the sky, dark and swollen with the threat of rain, though no drops had yet fallen.

The land around her was wild and untamed, a far cry from the city she had left behind. Tall grasses brushed against her legs as she walked, their tips swaying gently in the wind, while gnarled trees dotted the horizon, their twisted branches reaching skyward like claws. The scent of damp earth filled the air, mingling with the faint smell of woodsmoke drifting from the distant mountain villages.

Despite the beauty of the landscape, there was an undercurrent of unease that Red Mist couldn't ignore. The wind felt colder than it should, carrying with it whispers that seemed to come from the very land itself. Every rustle of leaves, every creak of branches made her hand twitch toward the hilt of her blade.

Her path led her along the edge of a dense forest, its towering trees casting long, jagged shadows across the ground. The trunks were thick with moss, and the canopy above was so tightly woven that only slivers of sunlight managed to pierce through, dappling the forest floor in a patchwork of light and shadow. In the distance, the mountains loomed, their peaks obscured by swirling clouds that clung stubbornly to the slopes.

Red Mist had traveled these roads before, but today the land felt different—tainted. The usual sense of tranquility that came with being out in the wilderness had been replaced by something darker, something lurking just beyond the edge of perception.

As she approached the entrance to a narrow ravine, the feeling of being watched grew stronger. She paused, her senses on high alert, her eyes narrowing as she scanned the area. The ravine was narrow, the rocky walls on either side rising steeply, casting deep shadows that seemed to shift and move with the wind. The path ahead was barely wide enough for two people to walk side by side, the ground uneven with loose stones and tangled roots.

It was here that she sensed it.

A presence—faint but unmistakable. It moved with the wind, a whisper of malice that seemed to curl around her like the fog that clung to the trees.

Red Mist's hand instinctively went to her katana, her fingers tightening around the hilt as she stepped forward. Her eyes scanned the rocky walls of the ravine, searching for the source of the presence she felt creeping toward her. The air had grown colder, the wind picking up, carrying with it the faint scent of rot and decay.

And then she saw it.

At the base of one of the rocky outcroppings, nestled in the shadow of a towering tree, was a creature—an old, twisted spirit. Its body was hunched and gnarled like the roots of an ancient tree, its skin a sickly gray-green, mottled with patches of dirt and moss. Its limbs were long and thin, its fingers clawed and sharp, digging into the earth as if it were part of the land itself. Its face was gaunt, its eyes hollow and sunken, glowing faintly with a malevolent light.

Red Mist had encountered jami before—wicked mountain spirits that lingered in places where the veil between the living and the dead was thin. They were dangerous, known for their cunning and malice, but this one seemed different. Weaker. It clung to the ground, its form barely holding together, as though it had been worn down by years of isolation and neglect.

The jami's hollow eyes fixed on her, and a rasping sound filled the air as it drew a breath, its chest heaving with the effort. Its gaze was cold, calculating, but there was a flicker of recognition in its sunken eyes. It knew who she was. Or what she was.

"Kōken..." the jami hissed, its voice low and grating, like stones grinding together. "So long since I have seen one of your kind."

Red Mist stood her ground, her hand steady on her blade. "What are you doing here?"

The jami's lips twisted into a cruel smile, though it didn't move from its place on the ground. "I am always here. Watching. Waiting."

"For what?"

The spirit's eyes darkened, its voice lowering to a whisper. "For the mountain to bleed again. For the shadows to return."

Red Mist's grip tightened. She had heard enough cryptic warnings over the years to know when a spirit was playing games, but there was something in the jami's words that struck her—a truth buried beneath the malice.

"What do you know of the darkness spreading across the city?" she asked, her voice steady but firm.

The jami's eyes gleamed with something like amusement. "The darkness has always been here, Kōken. It waits, in the cracks of the earth, in the shadows of the trees. But now..." The creature's voice trailed off, a thin, rasping breath escaping its lips. "Now, something has stirred it."

Red Mist narrowed her eyes. "What has stirred it?"

The jami let out a low, hollow laugh, its fingers digging deeper into the earth. "You will see soon enough, Kōken. The mountain is waking. The shadows are hungry."

With that, the jami's form began to fade, its body crumbling into dust, dissolving into the earth as if it had never been there at all. Only the faint echo of its words remained, lingering in the cold, still air.

Red Mist stood for a moment, her eyes scanning the ravine, but the spirit was gone.

The mountain is waking. The shadows are hungry.

Whatever was happening here, it was more than just restless spirits. Something older, something darker was stirring. And Red Mist intended to find out what it was.

後見

The wind had grown colder as Red Mist ventured deeper into the mountains, and the oppressive weight of malevolence hung heavily in the air. The path led her through twisted trees and jagged rocks, each step taking her further from the living world and deeper into a place where the past still lingered—angry and restless.

The ruins of the village came into view suddenly, as though they had been waiting for her behind the veil of trees. The once-thriving settlement had been reduced to little more than crumbling stone walls and the charred remains of buildings. The air was thick with the scent of ash, despite the decades that had passed since the village had been consumed by fire. Grass and weeds had overtaken the paths, but the village felt anything but abandoned. The malevolence that clung to this place was palpable, as though the very land had soaked up the horror of what had happened here.

Red Mist's eyes narrowed as she stepped cautiously through the remains of the village. The silence was unnerving, broken only by the occasional groan of the wind as it wound through the broken buildings. Shadows clung to the corners, and though she saw no movement, she couldn't shake the feeling that she wasn't alone.

As she moved deeper into the ruins, something caught her attention—a figure, small and still, sitting on the front steps of a ruined home. It was the spirit of a young girl.

The girl sat quietly, her hands resting in her lap, holding something close to her chest. Her form was faint, almost translucent, but there was no mistaking the sadness that radiated from her. Her head was bowed, her long hair falling over her face, obscuring her features. She didn't move, didn't acknowledge Red Mist's presence.

Red Mist hesitated, her hand instinctively hovering over the hilt of her katana. The girl wasn't moving, wasn't making a sound, but there was something deeply unsettling about the way she sat there, as if frozen in time. The malevolence in the air seemed to thicken around the girl, wrapping her in an aura of cold despair.

Slowly, Red Mist approached, her footsteps light on the crumbling ground.

"Who are you?" Red Mist asked, her voice low but firm.

The girl didn't respond. She remained perfectly still, her head still bowed, her hands gripping whatever she was holding close to her chest. The wind howled softly through the ruins, carrying with it the faint echo of distant screams, barely audible but unmistakable.

Red Mist took another step forward, her eyes never leaving the girl's ghostly form. "What happened here?"

Still, the girl remained silent.

The tension in the air grew heavier with each step, like a tightening noose. Red Mist could feel the malevolence pulsing from the girl, as if the spirit was somehow connected to the horrors that had taken place in the village long ago. She moved closer, her gaze flickering down to what the girl was holding in her lap.

It was a doll. A small, ragged doll, its clothes worn and dirtied by time, its button eyes staring blankly ahead. The girl clutched the doll tightly, as though it were the only thing keeping her tethered to this place.

Red Mist's heart quickened, but she kept her face calm, her movements slow. She was only a few steps away now, close enough to see the faint outline of the girl's face through her tangled hair.

"Can you hear me?" Red Mist asked again, her voice softer this time. "I can help you."

But the girl didn't respond. She sat, motionless, the silence pressing down around them like a shroud.

Red Mist reached out, her hand trembling slightly as she moved to place it on the girl's shoulder. Just as her fingers grazed the ghostly form, the girl's head twisted toward her with a sharp, unnatural motion. The snap of the movement was sudden, jarring, and Red Mist froze as she found herself staring into the girl's eyes—black and hollow.

The world around her vanished.

Red Mist was no longer standing in the ruined village. Instead, she found herself surrounded by flames, the sky above choked with thick, black smoke. The village was burning, consumed by a raging inferno, its buildings collapsing into piles of smoldering rubble. The air was thick with the acrid smell of ash and burning flesh, and the screams of the villagers echoed loudly in her ears—desperate, terrified cries that tore through the roar of the fire.

Red Mist staggered back, her heart pounding as she tried to make sense of what she was seeing. The flames licked at her skin, though she felt no pain. The ground beneath her was cracked and blackened, the earth split open as if the very land had been torn apart.

In the distance, she saw them—figures, or was it only one being, monstrous and towering, moving through the flames. Eyes glowed with a crimson light, the massive form hunched and twisted as it stalked through the burning village, cutting down anyone in their its. The creature, broad and covered in jagged, charred scales, its eyes burning with hatred, let out a roar that shook the earth.

An akuma.

The destruction was absolute. Men, women, and children ran in every direction, but there was no escape. The air was thick with the stench of death, and the sky above was darkened by the smoke and the shadow of the creature that ravaged the village.

Red Mist's breath came in ragged gasps as she watched the scene unfold. She could feel the terror, the helplessness of the villagers as they were slaughtered, as their lives were torn apart by forces they couldn't comprehend. The fire, the destruction, the screams—it was all-consuming.

Suddenly, the vision shifted. Red Mist found herself back in front of the ruined home, standing where the girl had been sitting. The world was silent, the flames gone, replaced by the cold, eerie stillness of the ruins. But the weight of the destruction lingered in the air, a malevolent presence that hadn't left with the fire.

The girl was gone.

Red Mist blinked, her mind reeling from the intensity of the vision. She looked down at her hands, still trembling slightly from the experience. The village was quiet once more, the only sound the distant rustling of leaves in the wind. She glanced at the spot where the spirit of the girl had been sitting, but there was nothing there now. No trace of her except for the doll.

The small, ragged doll lay on the ground where the girl had been, but now its faded clothes were charred and bloodied. The button eyes were still there, staring up at Red Mist, but they were burned, melted slightly from the heat of the flames.

Red Mist knelt down, her hand hovering over the doll for a moment before she picked it up. The fabric was rough against her skin, and as she held it, she could feel the weight of what had happened here. The doll was a reminder, a relic of the horrors that had taken place long ago.

She stood, the doll still in her hand, her gaze drifting over the ruins of the village. Whatever had happened here, the malevolence that lingered was not of this world. The spirits of this place were restless, and the darkness that had consumed them had not yet left.

The vision had shown her what had happened, but it hadn't given her answers—only more questions. And the sense of dread that filled her chest told her that the darkness that had destroyed this village was still out there, waiting to strike again.

六

THE STREETS OF SANPUKU were familiar yet different to Wakamono. He had spent years navigating these bustling alleys, but now, the weight of the spreading darkness seemed to press down on the city like a heavy cloak. The people moved about their business, but there was a nervous energy in their steps, and Wakamono couldn't help but feel the tension in the air.

His destination, however, was a place of comfort. Mr. Jin's supply shop had been a constant presence in his life since he first arrived in Sanpuku City, seeking shelter. The old wooden sign hanging above the door, weathered but still sturdy, read: *Jin's Wholesale Supply – Meat, Fish, Produce*. It wasn't a fancy establishment, but it was one that had earned the trust of countless restaurant owners and chefs throughout the city.

Wakamono paused in front of the door, taking a deep breath before stepping inside.

The scent of fresh produce and salted fish hit him immediately, along with the faint tang of dried herbs and the earthy smell of crates stacked with vegetables. The front of the shop was cluttered with boxes of goods ready for delivery, and the familiar low murmur of activity came from the back, where Mr. Jin likely was, overseeing the packing of an order.

"Wakamono!" Mrs. Jin's voice cut through the stillness like a bright note, filled with warmth and joy. She emerged from behind a counter, wiping her hands on an apron dusted with flour. "Look at you! It's been so long!"

Before he could respond, Mrs. Jin was already wrapping him in a tight embrace. She was as energetic as ever, her small frame bustling with life. Wakamono smiled, letting himself relax as she fussed over him, tugging at his sleeve and patting his shoulder.

"You've grown so much," she said, stepping back to get a good look at him. "I told Mr. Jin you'd be fine out there, didn't I?"

Wakamono chuckled. "It's good to see you, Mrs. Jin. I've been meaning to visit for a while."

"Well, you're here now," she said with a wink. "I bet you're hungry, too. Let me get you something."

Before Wakamono could respond, she had already disappeared into the back, leaving him standing in the middle of the shop, feeling a warmth in his chest he hadn't felt in a while.

A moment later, Mr. Jin emerged from the back room, carrying a crate of fresh fish. He set it down with practiced ease before turning to Wakamono, his usual stoic expression softening just slightly as he took in the sight of the young man who had once been under his care.

"Wakamono," Mr. Jin said with a nod. "Good to see you."

Wakamono smiled and bowed slightly. "It's good to see you too, Mr. Jin. It's been too long."

Mr. Jin's gaze lingered on him for a moment, his eyes scanning Wakamono's face as if searching for signs of change. "You've been busy," he said after a pause. "Looks like it's been good for you."

"It has," Wakamono replied, though his tone was a bit more serious than he intended. "How have things been here? Business as usual?"

Mr. Jin nodded, glancing around the shop. "Business is steady. The restaurants still need their supplies, and I make sure they get them."

Wakamono noticed the slight furrow in Mr. Jin's brow, the subtle way his gaze shifted, as if he too had felt the changes in the air. It wasn't just business as usual. Something was weighing on him, even if he wouldn't admit it outright.

Before he could ask further, Mrs. Jin returned with a small plate of food—some grilled fish and pickled vegetables. "Here you go, dear. You must be starving."

Wakamono thanked her and took a bite, the familiar flavors reminding him of simpler times. As he ate, the small talk continued—catching up on the goings-on in the shop, reminiscing about the days when Wakamono had first arrived in the city. But the unease in Wakamono's chest grew with each passing minute, and he knew he couldn't delay the reason for his visit much longer.

He set the plate down, his gaze drifting toward the front of the shop. "Mr. Jin, Mrs. Jin... there's something I need to talk to you about."

Mrs. Jin glanced at her husband, her hands stilling as she waited for Wakamono to continue.

"I've been... seeing things," Wakamono said slowly, choosing his words carefully. "The city isn't the same. Something dark is spreading, and I've seen the effects of it. People are scared. And it's not just rumors—it's real. I'm worried for your safety here."

Mr. Jin didn't say anything for a moment, his expression unreadable, but Wakamono could see the wheels turning in his mind. Mrs. Jin, on the other hand, frowned, her concern immediately evident.

"We've noticed things, too," Mrs. Jin said quietly. "People acting strange, whispers of things happening at night. But what can we do? This is our home. Our business."

Mr. Jin finally spoke, his voice steady but firm. "We've lived through hard times before, Wakamono. This city has seen its share of trouble. But we've built our life here. We can't just walk away from that."

Wakamono felt a surge of frustration rise in his chest, but he pushed it down. He knew they were right in their own way, but the danger was too real, too immediate for him to ignore.

"I understand," he said, his voice calm despite the tension. "But I'm worried it's going to get worse. I don't want you to be caught in the middle of it. You have to be careful."

Mr. Jin met his gaze, his expression softening just slightly. "We appreciate the warning, Wakamono. But leaving isn't an option. This is everything we have."

Mrs. Jin placed a hand on Wakamono's arm, her touch gentle but resolute. "We'll be all right, dear. Don't worry about us."

Wakamono wanted to argue, to tell them just how serious the danger was, but he knew it wouldn't change their minds. They were as stubborn as ever, and no amount of warning would make them abandon their life here.

"Just promise me you'll stay safe," Wakamono said finally. "If things get worse, don't hesitate to leave."

Mr. Jin nodded, though the determined set of his jaw told Wakamono they would stay until the very end.

"We'll be here," Mr. Jin said simply.

Wakamono stood, bowing slightly as he prepared to leave. "I'll check in on you."

Mrs. Jin smiled warmly. "You do that. And make sure you eat more. You're still too skinny!"

With that, Wakamono stepped out into the streets of Sanpuku once more, the weight of his concern pressing heavily on his shoulders. He couldn't shake the feeling that no matter how hard he tried, he couldn't protect everyone.

後見

The Kōken facility was eerily quiet, the usual hum of life absent as Wakamono entered its halls. Red Mist still hadn't returned, and the emptiness only deepened the restlessness gnawing at him. The walls felt too close, the silence too heavy. He needed to move, to channel the tension coiling inside him into something tangible.

Without hesitation, Wakamono made his way to the training hall, the familiar scent of wood and sweat calming him slightly. He shrugged off his cloak and stretched his arms, feeling the muscles tense under his skin. His katana gleamed faintly in the dim light, and he drew it with a practiced, fluid motion, the sound of steel against its sheath a brief comfort.

He stepped into the center of the room, his bare feet sliding into position on the smooth wooden floor. His body moved instinctively into the first stance—feet wide, knees bent, katana raised. For a moment, he let himself breathe, his eyes closing as he focused on the weight of the blade in his hands, the cool air against his skin.

Focus, he told himself. *Control.*

The first strike was swift, cutting through the air with a sharp whistle. His arms extended fully, his movements precise, honed by hours of practice. He pivoted smoothly into the next form, his feet gliding over the floor as he slashed again, the blade slicing an invisible enemy. Each motion was deliberate, every step calculated.

But his mind refused to quiet.

Images flashed behind his eyes—the faces of the people in the city. Mr. and Mrs. Jin, standing in their shop, stubbornly determined to stay. The market vendors he passed by earlier, their eyes betraying their fear despite their attempts to continue with their daily lives. Children running through the streets, oblivious to the dark cloud that seemed to be creeping over the city.

His grip tightened on the hilt of the katana as he swung again, harder this time, the blade cutting a sharper arc through the air. He could feel his heart pounding in his chest, his breath coming in short bursts as he moved into the next form.

I can't protect them all.

The thought struck him harder than any blow. He pivoted into another stance, but his mind was already spiraling. The darkness was spreading—he had seen it in the empty streets, in the whispered conversations, in the way people glanced over their shoulders as if expecting something to strike at any moment. And there was nothing he could do to stop it.

He swung again, faster, his muscles burning as he pushed himself harder. Each strike was more aggressive than the last, as though he could drive the thoughts out of his mind through sheer force. But no matter how hard he trained, no matter how sharp his movements, the weight of his helplessness remained.

The spirits are growing stronger, he thought, his katana cutting through the air in another sweeping arc. *Every day, they're getting bolder. And we're not ready.*

His breath came faster, his body moving with a frantic energy that mirrored the chaos in his mind. He could see the spirits—the ones that had attacked, the ones that lingered at the edges of the city, watching. The people in the city had no idea what was coming. Not fully. And those who did were too scared to leave, too tied to their lives to abandon them.

Another strike. His arms were trembling now, the weight of the katana heavy in his hands.

Mr. Jin. Mrs. Jin. He swung again, his form faltering slightly. *The merchants. The citizens of Sanpuku. The children.* He couldn't protect them all. He wasn't strong enough.

He forced his body into another stance, his muscles screaming in protest. His vision blurred slightly from the exertion, but he didn't stop. He couldn't. If he stopped, the thoughts would overwhelm him.

His blade continued to cut through the air, the motions sharp, but unsteady.

I need to be stronger.

His legs were shaking now, his breath ragged as he struggled to maintain control. His body was reaching its limit, but his mind was still racing, still caught in the spiral of fear and frustration. He could feel the malevolence spreading over the city, like a dark shadow creeping through the streets, slipping into people's homes, their minds.

The spirits were coming. And behind them, something worse.

He gritted his teeth, forcing his body into another form, but his movements were sloppy now, the fluidity gone. His mind was unraveling, and with it, the precision of his training.

What if Red Mist doesn't come back?

The thought hit him like a blow to the chest. His foot slipped, his balance faltering as he swung the katana wildly, the blade striking the floor with a loud crack. He froze, his breath ragged, his body trembling from the exertion. For a moment, the silence of the training hall pressed down on him, and he could hear nothing but the sound of his own heartbeat pounding in his ears.

He was losing control.

Wakamono stood still, the katana hanging limply in his hand as he struggled to steady his breathing. Sweat dripped down his face, his muscles aching from the intensity of the session. He closed his eyes, trying to calm his racing thoughts, but the fear and doubt clung to him like a second skin.

I'm not ready.

He gripped the hilt of the katana tighter, frustration and fear warring inside him. He had trained for this—trained to protect, to fight. But what good was it if he couldn't even keep his own mind in check? How was he supposed to protect the city if he couldn't protect himself?

His breath slowed, but the tension in his chest remained. He lifted the katana again, preparing to continue, to force himself back into control, but before he could move, a soft sound caught his attention.

The faint creak of a door opening.

He turned, his heart skipping a beat as he saw her standing at the entrance to the training hall—Red Mist. Her presence was calm, controlled, as always, though there was a heaviness in her eyes that hadn't been there before.

For a moment, neither of them spoke.

Red Mist's gaze flickered to the katana in Waka-mono's hand, then back to his face. She could see the exhaustion in his eyes, the frustration, the fear. But she said nothing.

She didn't need to.

Red Mist stepped into the training hall, her presence calm but weighted with the events of the day. Wakamono watched her closely, the tension in his body slowly easing, though his mind still raced with questions.

He took a deep breath, lowering his katana. "Did you find anything useful?"

Red Mist moved closer, her eyes holding a depth of thought as she considered how to explain. "Some," she said quietly, though there was hesitation in her voice. "But not as much as I would have liked."

Wakamono sheathed his katana, his anxiety still simmering just beneath the surface. "What happened?"

Red Mist's gaze shifted, her mind briefly returning to the ruins of the village, the image of the spirit girl sitting on the steps with the doll. "I went further into the mountains," she began, her tone steady. "Most of what I encountered was unremarkable—spirits, lingering but harmless. Until I came across the ruins of an old village."

Wakamono's brow furrowed as he listened, sensing that this was where the true story lay.

"There was something... off about the place," Red Mist continued, her voice soft but firm. "The air was thick with malevolence, and it felt like the village had been frozen in the moment of its destruction. And then, I saw a young girl, sitting in front of what was left of a home, holding a doll."

Wakamono's stomach twisted. "A spirit?"

Red Mist nodded. "She didn't speak. Didn't move. But there was something about her presence that felt wrong. As I approached, she stayed silent... until her head twisted toward me, and I was cast into a vision." She paused, her eyes hardening slightly as she recalled the intensity of the experience. "I saw the destruction of the village. Fire. Death. A slaughter. It was as though I was standing in the middle of it, watching it happen."

Wakamono swallowed, his fists clenching slightly. "What... what caused it?"

Red Mist shook her head, a flicker of uncertainty crossing her face. "I'm not sure. It felt like something... ancient. Powerful. Maybe and akuma."

"And the girl?"

"When the vision ended, she was gone," Red Mist said quietly. "All that was left was the doll she had been holding, bloodied and charred." She exhaled slowly, her gaze meeting Wakamono's. "Whatever happened in that village, it's tied to the malevolence spreading through the city. I just don't know how yet."

Wakamono was silent for a moment, trying to process what she had told him. The weight of the unknown hung between them, thick and suffocating.

"And you? What did you find?" Red Mist asked, breaking the silence.

Wakamono ran a hand through his hair, feeling the familiar frustration bubble up again. "Not much. The archives are full of old scrolls, but nothing that really made sense. I found one that seemed like it might be important—it had symbols for 'watching' and 'burning' and the eyes I have been seeing. But I couldn't fully decipher it. I went to see a historian, but..." He hesitated, remembering Shiki's cryptic demeanor. "S he's... working on it."

Red Mist raised an eyebrow. "Do you trust her?"

Wakamono shrugged. "She's eccentric, but she seems to know what she's doing. She told me to come back tomorrow." He frowned. "But I don't know if it's going to be enough."

Red Mist nodded thoughtfully, her fingers brushing the hilt of her own katana. "We're running out of time," she said quietly. "The city is on the brink. If we don't find answers soon..."

She didn't finish the sentence, but the weight of her words hung in the air between them.

Wakamono's chest tightened as he looked at her. "What do we do now?"

Red Mist's gaze was steady, though there was a flicker of something uncertain in her eyes. "We keep searching. We follow every lead, no matter how small. The answers are out there, Wakamono. We just have to find them before it's too late."

七

THE NARROW STREETS OF Sanpuku felt colder than usual as Wakamono and Red Mist approached the historian's home. The sun hung low in the sky, casting long shadows across the stone path. Wakamono's steps were brisk, his mind still racing with the tension of the past few days. Beside him, Red Mist moved with her usual calm, though Wakamono could sense the weight of her thoughts.

When they reached Shiki's door, Wakamono knocked firmly. A faint rustle came from inside, followed by the sound of footsteps. The door creaked open, revealing the historian's thin frame. Her eyes, sharp despite her age, flickered with recognition.

"Ah, you're back," Shiki said, her voice dry and faintly amused. "Come in, come in. I've been expecting you."

Wakamono exchanged a glance with Red Mist before stepping inside. The scent of old paper and incense filled the air, and the small room was just as cluttered as before—books stacked haphazardly on shelves, scrolls unrolled across the table, and strange trinkets hanging from the ceiling beams.

Shiki closed the door behind them and gestured toward a low table in the corner, where a single, weathered scroll lay unfurled. "I assume you're eager to hear what I've uncovered."

Wakamono and Red Mist sat across from her, the tension in the room thickening. Shiki didn't waste time with pleasantries. She moved to the scroll and tapped it lightly with one bony finger.

"This," she began, "is not just a collection of old symbols and forgotten stories. It's the account of a destruction—a warning, if you will." Her eyes gleamed as she glanced at Wakamono. "A warning about an akuma."

Wakamono felt a chill crawl down his spine, and he leaned in closer. "What kind of akuma?"

Shiki's lips twisted into a grim smile. "One you may have already felt the shadow of. The scroll speaks of a nearby village—now long gone—that was utterly destroyed by a creature of unspeakable power. Its name, though rarely spoken aloud anymore, is Onkai."

Red Mist's expression didn't change, but her eyes darkened. "Onkai. I've heard whispers of it before."

Shiki nodded. "Most Kōken have. But few know the full story." She traced her finger along the symbols etched into the scroll, her voice lowering as if the very words carried a curse. "Onkai is an akuma of immense power, one that thrives on suffering. According to the scroll, it arrived without warning, drawn to the village by... well, no one knows for certain what attracted it. But when it came, it brought only devastation. The village was wiped out in a single night—its people slaughtered, their homes reduced to ash."

Wakamono's heart pounded in his chest. He had seen destruction before, but this sounded like something beyond anything he could imagine. "The omens we've seen in the city... are they like what happened before Onkai attacked the village?"

Shiki's eyes flicked to him, her gaze sharp. "Very similar. The scroll describes strange occurrences—unexplained deaths, animals going mad, crops withering in hours. And then, the night before the attack, there were whispers on the wind, voices of the dead calling from the shadows." She paused, her face growing serious. "Sound familiar?"

Wakamono clenched his fists. He again thought of Mr. and Mrs. Jin, of the market vendors and the children in the streets. He had seen those same omens in Sanpuku—the strange glances, the whispers of fear. "It's happening."

Shiki sighed, her fingers resting on the edge of the scroll. "It seems so. I don't believe this is a coincidence. Onkai is drawn to places of life and energy, and once it arrives, it leaves nothing but destruction in its wake."

Red Mist, who had been silent until now, leaned forward slightly. "What exactly is Onkai? The scroll mentions destruction, but it doesn't describe what kind of creature we're dealing with."

Shiki shook her head slowly. "The details are vague. The people who survived the this sighting were too young or didn't last long enough to give a proper account. All the scrolls say is that it is a force of chaos and torment, something that feeds off pain. I did find more about it in other sources, but..." Her voice trailed off, and she glanced toward the stack of books at the far end of the room. "I'll get to that in a moment."

Wakamono's mind raced. The destruction of the village in the scroll, the strange occurrences happening now in Sanpuku—it was all connected. The malevolent spirits, the unsettling atmosphere. This wasn't just a passing threat. It was something much worse.

He exchanged a glance with Red Mist, who gave a barely perceptible nod. They had suspected something like this, but hearing it confirmed sent a shiver down his spine.

Shiki stood, moving to the stack of books. "But first, let me show you what else I found."

Shiki's home was dimly lit, the shadows cast by the flickering lanterns adding to the weight of the conversation. As Wakamono and Red Mist settled in, Shiki wasted no time. Her hands already rested on an open, weathered book at the center of the table. Its pages were thick with age, and on the yellowed parchment, drawings of creatures and dark symbols lined the margins.

"I've already done some digging into Onkai," Shiki began, her voice low but steady. "This is one of the few records I have on akuma, and it contains one of the only detailed accounts of Onkai. A creature feared for centuries."

She pointed to the large, ominous illustration in the middle of the page. Wakamono leaned in, his breath catching as he took in the sight. The depiction was nightmarish: Onkai was massive, its hunched body covered in jagged, charred scales. Its arms, ending in long, dripping claws, were outstretched as if to tear apart anything in its path. Most unsettling were the creature's eyes, two deep pits of hatred, glowing faintly from the shadows of its distorted face.

"This is the beast," Shiki continued. "Onkai. It's been called 'the Demon of Pain,' among other things. This akuma thrives on destruction and suffering. Where it goes, entire villages are wiped from existence. Its body is built for chaos—scales impervious to most weapons, claws that drip with corrosive ooze that melts anything it touches."

Wakamono felt a chill crawl up his spine. The stories of malevolent spirits in the city paled in comparison to what Shiki was describing. Onkai wasn't just a spirit—it was a force of pure destruction, seemingly unstoppable.

Red Mist studied the image with her usual calm demeanor, but her silence spoke volumes. She knew the gravity of what they were up against.

"How do we stop something like that?" Wakamono asked, his voice tense.

Shiki's lips pressed into a thin line. "The texts don't offer much in the way of solutions. It seems that few who encountered Onkai lived to tell the tale. Its scales are nearly impenetrable, and even if you do manage to wound it, its pain only seems to fuel its power. The more suffering it causes, the stronger it becomes."

Wakamono's frustration surged. "So, we just wait for it to tear through Sanpuku like that village in the scroll?"

"No," Red Mist said, her voice steady but firm. "We'll prepare. We know it's coming, which gives us some advantage. We need to understand its patterns—how it moves, where it strikes first. If it feeds on fear and suffering, we should continue to eliminate or drive away the rogue spirits in the city."

Shiki nodded, flipping through a few more pages. "Onkai doesn't arrive randomly. It follows a pattern, drawn to places of life and energy. It thrives in places like Sanpuku, where the population is large, and the fear is palpable. The strange occurrences you've seen—the spirits, the strange behavior in the city—those are signs that Onkai's presence is already having an effect."

Wakamono felt a knot form in his stomach. The quiet streets, the nervous glances of the people in the market, the inexplicable tension in the air—it all suddenly made sense. Sanpuku wasn't just a target; it was a feast for the akuma.

"Why here? Why now?" Wakamono asked, unable to contain his frustration. "Is there a reason it's coming to Sanpuku?"

Shiki shook her head slowly. "There's no clear reason why Onkai chooses one place over another. It's drawn to suffering and chaos. It could be the unrest in the city, the growing fear, the very life force of the people. What we do know is that once Onkai is here, it will leave nothing behind but ash and pain."

Silence settled over the room, heavy with the weight of the revelation. Wakamono clenched his fists. The people in Sanpuku—the citizens, the children, the Jins—they had no idea what was coming. And now, it felt as if they were running out of time.

"We need more information," Red Mist said, her voice cutting through the silence. "There must be something we're missing. Something that could give us an edge."

Shiki's expression softened. "I've told you all that I could find. The rest... I'm afraid you'll have to learn through experience."

Wakamono's jaw tightened. He hated the feeling of helplessness that gnawed at him. He wasn't ready for this—none of them were.

"We'll figure it out," Red Mist said, her tone offering no room for doubt. "We always do."

Shiki nodded, though her eyes carried a deep, unspoken worry. "Be careful, Kōken. Onkai's strength is not the only thing you'll face. Spirits are drawn to its presence, lesser evils that will amplify the chaos. You're not just fighting one demon—you're fighting a tide of darkness."

Wakamono exchanged a glance with Red Mist, the weight of their task settling even more heavily on his shoulders. But Red Mist's expression remained calm, unwavering.

"We'll face it," she said simply.

The weight of Shiki's words hung in the air as Wakamono and Red Mist exchanged glances. They had come for answers, but the information they'd received left more questions—questions that came with no clear solution.

Shiki closed the old tome gently, her hands lingering on the worn cover for a moment before she turned to face them both. "Onkai's presence will tear through the city," she said softly. "It's only a matter of time. If the omens are any indication, you don't have long before he reveals himself."

Red Mist's jaw tightened, her face a mask of calm determination. "We need to focus on preparing the city. There are too many people here who have no idea what's coming."

Wakamono, still reeling from the description of Onkai, clenched his fists. "How do we even start preparing for something like this? We don't even know where he'll strike first."

Red Mist remained focused. "We start by getting the city's defenses ready. If Onkai thrives on chaos, we need to limit the damage before he can fuel himself. Evacuate as many people as we can. The rest... we'll hold the line until we find a way to stop him."

Shiki frowned, the deep lines in her face etched with concern. "It won't be enough. Onkai's power grows with every moment of suffering. The more destruction, the more pain he causes, the stronger he becomes. He's more than just a physical threat. He feeds on the very terror that's already gripping this city."

Wakamono's heart pounded in his chest. The weight of responsibility was crushing. He thought of the people he had seen earlier—ordinary people going about their lives, unaware of the danger that was creeping closer. The thought of them being helpless against something like Onkai was unbearable.

Red Mist looked at him, her gaze steady but unreadable. "We'll find a way."

Wakamono nodded, though he felt the cold grip of uncertainty tightening around him. He couldn't shake the feeling that they were missing something, that despite their preparation, they would still be caught off guard.

"I'll stay here," Shiki said, her voice softer now. "I'll keep looking through my texts, see if I can find anything else that could help you. But you need to act fast."

Red Mist nodded. "We will."

The room fell silent for a moment, the weight of the impending battle pressing down on them all. Wakamono's mind raced, struggling to piece together what they could do. How do you fight something that grows stronger with each passing moment of pain?

Suddenly, the quiet of the room was shattered by a distant, muffled scream.

Wakamono's head jerked toward the door, his senses immediately on high alert. The sound of footsteps—hurried, frantic—followed by the unmistakable clamor of panicked voices began to echo from the streets outside.

Red Mist was already on her feet, her hand resting on the hilt of her katana. Wakamono followed, his pulse quickening as he moved toward the window. His stomach dropped as he looked out.

The city was in chaos.

People ran through the streets, their faces pale with terror. The distant sound of something heavy crashing echoed through the air, followed by more screams. In the distance, a dark plume of smoke rose into the sky, twisting ominously against the evening light.

"Something's happening," Wakamono said, his voice tight with urgency.

Red Mist didn't hesitate. She moved to the door, her expression hardening with resolve. "Let's go."

Wakamono rushed after her, the fear and adrenaline mixing in his veins. They couldn't afford to waste a single moment. Whatever was happening, it was the first sign that Onkai was coming.

As Red Mist pushed open the door, the sounds of the city's panic grew louder, the air thick with fear and confusion. They stepped into the street, the chaos unfolding around them.

Wakamono's eyes darted from one panicked figure to the next, searching for the source of the terror. The distant crash came again, and this time he could feel it—a deep, unsettling tremor in the ground beneath his feet.

"It's starting," Red Mist said, her voice barely audible over the clamor.

Wakamono's heart raced as they moved quickly down the street, the darkening sky above them casting long shadows over the city. He couldn't help but feel that they were too late—that the destruction they had feared was already upon them.

8
八

THE STREETS OF SANPUKU were not quiet, but the sounds of the marketplace had changed. The usual chatter of merchants hawking their wares and the rhythmic clattering of carts along the cobbled streets had given way to something else—something darker. Panic had taken hold, a ripple of confusion and fear that spread through the marketplace like wildfire.

Near the center of the market, a merchant's cart, once laden with goods, stood ominously still. At first glance, it looked ordinary—its wooden frame worn with use, its wheels slightly crooked from years of travel through the streets. But something wasn't right. The air around it shimmered faintly, a crackling energy sparking from its surface. The wood creaked unnaturally, as though it were alive.

The merchant, who had been selling his goods just moments ago, stepped back, eyes wide with terror. The cart's frame groaned, its joints snapping and twisting in ways no inanimate object should. One wheel splintered, sending shards of wood scattering across the ground, and the merchant let out a startled shout, stumbling backward.

Onlookers began to gather, unsure of what they were witnessing. Whispers filled the air, confusion rippling through the crowd as the once-harmless cart buckled and warped. Its sides bulged outward, like something inside was trying to tear its way free. The merchant's goods spilled onto the cobblestones—sacks of rice, bundles of dried herbs—rolling away as the cart shuddered violently.

A hush fell over the crowd as the cart's transformation became undeniable. Its wooden frame twisted into a grotesque shape, jagged pieces of wood splintering outward like spikes. The metal fittings stretched and warped, becoming sharp edges that gleamed in the dim light. The cart's wheels, now cracked and splintered, dug into the ground, pulling the rest of the structure upright as if it were standing on legs.

It was no longer just a cart.

With a thunderous crack, the tsukumogami completed its transformation, rising to its full height. What had once been a tool of trade was now a hulking, nightmarish creature of twisted wood and metal, its jagged form hunched and dangerous. Its front wheels split and reformed into claw-like appendages, and the sacks of rice that had spilled earlier were now wrapped around its base, flailing like tendrils.

The crowd erupted into screams.

The tsukumogami lashed out, its newly formed limbs smashing into nearby stalls and scattering people in every direction. The ground shook as it moved, each step sending tremors through the market square. Wooden beams snapped like twigs under its blows, and the air filled with the sound of destruction.

From the shadows of a nearby alley, two figures emerged.

Red Mist and Wakamono arrived, their movements swift and calculated. The sound of the panic had drawn them there, and the sight of the tsukumogami now rampaging through the market confirmed their worst fears. The malevolent spirits of the city were waking up—and they were coming for everything.

Wakamono's heart raced as he sized up the creature. He had seen tsukumogami before, but nothing like this. This one was enormous, its grotesque form far more dangerous than the typical animated objects he had encountered in his training. Its long, jagged limbs tore through the air, sending debris flying as it swatted at the terrified crowd.

"Wakamono," Red Mist said sharply, her voice cutting through the chaos. "Stay focused."

Her calm demeanor was a sharp contrast to the panic around them, and Wakamono felt a surge of determination. He had fought alongside her before, but this was different. The stakes were higher, the danger more real.

He nodded, his hand instinctively gripping his katana. "Got it."

Red Mist moved first, her movements swift and precise. She darted forward, positioning herself between the tsukumogami and the fleeing civilians, her katana gleaming in the fading daylight. Wakamono followed her lead, taking up position on the opposite side of the creature, his heart pounding as he prepared for the battle ahead.

The tsukumogami roared, a deep, creaking sound that echoed through the square. Its wooden frame shuddered, its jagged limbs reaching for them as it charged. But Red Mist was faster. With a single fluid motion, she leaped forward, her katana slicing through one of the creature's claw-like appendages.

The tsukumogami let out a screech, staggering backward as splinters of wood scattered through the air. Wakamono saw his opening and lunged, his katana cutting through the creature's other limb. The impact sent a shockwave through his arms, but he held firm, driving the blade deeper into the creature's wooden body.

The creature flailed wildly, its twisted form buckling under the assault. But it wasn't done yet. With a violent swing of its remaining limbs, it lashed out, sending debris flying toward Red Mist. She dodged effortlessly, her movements a blur as she darted to the side, avoiding the deadly swing.

Wakamono followed her lead, his mind racing as he prepared for the next strike. They needed to end this quickly, before the creature caused more destruction—or worse, before more spirits began to awaken.

The tsukumogami roared again, the sound like wood splintering under immense pressure. Its misshapen limbs flailed wildly, sending shards of debris flying in every direction. Civilians scrambled to escape, ducking behind overturned stalls and fleeing toward the far edges of the square.

Wakamono's grip tightened on his katana. His breath came fast and heavy, his mind racing to keep up with the chaos around him. Red Mist had already moved, her figure a blur as she circled the creature with swift, practiced steps. Her focus was razor-sharp, her katana gleaming as she prepared for another strike.

Wakamono's eyes darted between her and the tsukumogami. He couldn't let his fear take control. He was stronger than that—Red Mist had taught him that. But the sheer size of the creature, its unpredictable swings and jagged, shifting form, sent a wave of uncertainty through him.

With a sharp exhale, he shook it off. He couldn't hesitate. Not now.

The tsukumogami lunged forward again, its wooden limbs crashing down with enough force to splinter the cobblestones beneath it. Wakamono reacted instinctively, throwing himself to the side as the creature's massive arm smashed into the ground where he'd just been standing. He felt the shockwave ripple through his legs as he rolled to his feet, heart pounding.

Red Mist was already there, her katana a blur of motion. She slashed at the creature's leg, her blade biting deep into the twisted wood. The tsukumogami screeched in fury, staggering backward as it tried to shake off the blow.

"Wakamono!" Red Mist's voice rang out, clear and commanding over the din of battle. "Focus on its core! Aim for where the wood is weakest."

Wakamono's eyes snapped to the center of the creature's body, where the wood was more gnarled and cracked. He could see it now—the weak spot in the tsukumogami's form, a place where the knots in the wood were less dense, more vulnerable.

He moved swiftly, dodging another wild swing from the creature as he closed in. His katana gleamed in the fading light as he struck, the blade slicing into the tsukumogami. The creature shrieked in pain, its massive frame convulsing as Wakamono drove his blade deeper.

The impact sent a jolt through Wakamono's arms, but he held firm, pushing the katana further into the creature's wooden body. The tsukumogami thrashed violently, its jagged limbs flailing as it tried to dislodge him, but Wakamono didn't let go.

Red Mist moved in tandem, her katana flashing as she struck the creature's other side, driving her blade into the base of its spine-like structure. The combined force of their attacks sent the tsukumogami staggering, its legs buckling under the strain.

With a final, guttural scream, the creature collapsed, its twisted form crashing to the ground in a heap of splintered wood and shattered metal. Wakamono leaped back, breathing hard, his heart still racing as he watched the tsukumogami's remains crumble into nothing more than debris.

The market square was eerily quiet now, the panicked screams of the civilians fading into the distance as the last of the tsukumogami's energy dissipated. The air was heavy with the scent of wood and dust, and for a moment, all Wakamono could hear was the sound of his own ragged breathing.

Red Mist straightened, her katana still in hand, though her expression remained calm and controlled. She glanced over at Wakamono, her eyes briefly flicking over his form as if assessing his condition.

"You held your ground," she said, her tone even. "Well done."

Wakamono nodded, though his hands still trembled slightly from the adrenaline. "Thanks."

Before either of them could catch their breath, the sound of heavy footsteps echoed through the narrow streets leading to the marketplace. Wakamono turned, his body tense, expecting another attack.

From the settling dust, a figure emerged.

The temperature seemed to drop as the figure glided into the square, its presence both ethereal and terrifying. The translucent form was dressed in the elaborate robes of a noble, but its face was twisted with rage, its eyes burning with an otherworldly fury.

Wakamono's breath caught in his throat as he recognized the vengeful spirit of a noble. He had heard stories of the goryō—spirits who had died in anger and now sought revenge on the living. They were powerful, and far more dangerous than the tsukumogami they had just faced.

The goryō's form hovered above the ground, its gaze locked onto a group of terrified civilians huddled behind an overturned stall. Its expression was one of pure hatred, and Wakamono could feel the heavy, oppressive aura radiating from it. This spirit wasn't here by chance. It was drawn by the chaos, by the fear coursing through the city.

Red Mist moved first.

Without hesitation, she darted forward, her katana raised. Wakamono followed her lead, his mind racing.

They couldn't afford to let the goryō wreak havoc on the already-panicked civilians.

The goryō hissed, its voice like wind whipping through dead trees, and with a single gesture, it sent a blast of energy toward Red Mist and Wakamono. They both dove to the side, barely avoiding the wave of dark energy as it exploded against the cobblestones, sending shards of stone flying in all directions.

Wakamono scrambled to his feet, his katana still in hand. The goryō turned its attention toward him, its eyes narrowing as it floated closer. His pulse quickened, the cold chill of the spirit's aura sending shivers down his spine.

"Stay sharp!" Red Mist called, her voice cutting through the fog of fear. "It's strong, but it can be defeated."

Wakamono nodded, his grip tightening on his sword as he prepared for the next strike. The goryō was unlike anything he had faced before, its movements swift and fluid, its power palpable. But he wasn't alone. He had Red Mist by his side.

The air was thick with the oppressive weight of the goryō's presence, its shrieking voice echoing across the market square. The ground trembled beneath their feet, cracks spreading through the cobblestones as the spirit's fury reached a fever pitch.

Red Mist and Wakamono had already struck at the goryō several times, but each blow barely made a dent in its ethereal form. Their blades passed through its flickering body like cutting through mist, leaving only faint ripples in the air. The spirit's translucent eyes glowed with rage, its entire form a swirling mass of vengeance and fury.

"I will tear this city apart!" the goryō screeched, its voice warped and angry. "They will know my suffering!"

Wakamono gritted his teeth, frustration gnawing at him as he struck at the goryō again, only to see his katana pass uselessly through its form. "It's not working!" he called out, his voice tight with strain.

Red Mist, more composed but equally determined, watched the goryō closely. Her sharp eyes scanned the battlefield, taking in every detail—the way the spirit recoiled from certain light, how it seemed to flicker more violently when they drew closer to certain objects in the marketplace. It was clear now that physical attacks alone wouldn't defeat it.

She took a deep breath, lowering her katana for a moment as a realization washed over her. "Wakamono," she called, her voice steady despite the chaos. "We cannot harm it with normal blades."

Wakamono blinked, unsure of what she meant at first, but he trusted her judgment. He watched as Red Mist knelt, placing her katana gently on the ground. With one hand resting on the hilt, she began to mutter an ancient arrangement of words—her voice soft but powerful, imbued with meaning.

> *Life flows through this blade,*
> *Roots of peace strike at the heart,*
> *Breath back to Seken.*

As the final words left her lips, a soft glow began to emanate from her katana, bathing the square in a faint, bluish light. The oppressive weight of the goryō's presence seemed to lift slightly, as if the spirit itself sensed the change in the air. Wakamono watched in awe as the glow intensified, the blade now humming with a power he had never seen before.

Red Mist stood, her eyes locked on the goryō, who recoiled at the sight of her glowing weapon. The spirit let out a low hiss, its form flickering as though it were losing control.

"Now," Red Mist commanded, her voice sharp. "It is vulnerable."

Wakamono nodded, his grip tightening on his katana as he moved in tandem with Red Mist. Together, they rushed the goryō from opposite sides, their blades raised. The spirit screamed, lashing out with wild tendrils of dark energy, but its attacks were less focused, more desperate.

Red Mist reached the goryō first, her glowing katana slashing through its form with a burst of spiritual energy. The spirit let out a shriek of pain as its body flickered violently, its translucent form unraveling. Wakamono seized the opportunity, darting forward and striking at the goryō from the other side. His blade didn't fracture the spirit like Red Mist's, but his precise movements kept it off balance.

The goryō wailed, its voice rising to an unbearable pitch as Red Mist closed in for the final blow. With fluid, graceful motion, she thrust her blade into the goryō's chest, twisted, her back to the spirit, and thrust her blade in an upward arch in one powerful motion. Her katana erupted through the goryō's chest and head, the glowing blade cutting its twisted form like a beacon of light in the darkness.

The goryō's scream of fury turned into a high-pitched wail as its body shattered, scattering dark matter across the marketplace. The black shards twinkled and dissipated in the air, leaving behind only the faintest traces of shadow as the goryō's presence faded completely.

For a moment, the marketplace was still, the echoes of the battle slowly fading into silence.

Wakamono stood frozen, his heart pounding in his chest as he watched the last of the spirit's remains vanish into nothingness. The cold, oppressive energy that had filled the air was gone, replaced by a strange, eerie calm.

Red Mist sheathed her glowing katana, her expression as composed as ever. "It's over," she said quietly, her eyes scanning the now-empty square. "For now."

Wakamono exhaled deeply, relief flooding through him, but his mind was still racing. He looked around, taking in the destruction that had been left in the goryō's wake—the overturned stalls, the cracks in the cobblestones, and the few shaken civilians who had taken cover during the fight.

"There's more out there," Wakamono said, his voice low. "More spirits. The city is still in danger."

Red Mist glanced at him, her eyes narrowing slightly. "We'll deal with them," she said, though there was a hint of weariness in her tone.

Wakamono's mind raced as he thought of the spreading chaos. They couldn't stay here and wait—there was too much ground to cover, too many threats appearing in every corner of the city.

"We should split up," Wakamono suggested, his tone urgent. "We can cover more ground that way. You take the north, I'll head south."

Red Mist's gaze lingered on him for a moment, her expression unreadable. She knew the danger they were facing—splitting up wasn't ideal, but Wakamono was right. There wasn't enough time to stay together.

Finally, she nodded, though there was a faint edge of reluctance in her voice. "Fine," she said quietly. "But don't die."

Wakamono gave her a tight nod, his determination clear in his eyes.

Without another word, they turned in opposite directions, each moving swiftly toward the next threat looming over Sanpuku. As Wakamono disappeared down the narrow streets, the weight of his task pressed heavily on his shoulders. But he wouldn't stop. Not until the city was safe.

九

THE STREETS OF SANPUKU were still teeming with chaos, but in a narrow alley just beyond the market square, a strange quiet had settled. It was the kind of silence that made the hair on the back of the neck stand up, a silence that whispered danger to anyone who ventured too close.

A young man hurried through the alley, his steps quick and nervous. He had heard the screams from the marketplace and knew the city was under attack, but he hadn't expected to stumble upon something far worse than the chaos outside the narrow passageway.

"Help... please..." The voice was soft, weak, barely more than a whisper. It came from deeper within the alley, hidden in the shadows.

The man froze in his tracks, his heart pounding in his chest. "Who's there?" he called, his voice shaking.

"Please... help me..."

He stepped closer, squinting to see through the dim light. As he approached, a figure came into view—a woman, slumped against the wall, her kimono torn, her long black hair covering her face. She was trembling, clutching her side as though in pain.

The man's heart ached at the sight of her. "Are you alright?" he asked, stepping toward her, his voice filled with concern.

The woman lifted her head slowly, revealing a pale, delicate face streaked with tears. Her lips trembled, and her eyes were wide with fear. "I... I was attacked," she said, her voice barely audible. "Please... I don't know what to do."

The frail creature's pleading drew him in—the way she looked at him, so vulnerable and helpless. He couldn't just leave her here.

He reached out a hand to help her. "It's okay," he said softly. "I'll get you to safety."

The woman's hand reached for his, but just as their fingers touched, her grip tightened unnaturally fast. The man's breath caught in his throat as he realized too late that something was terribly wrong.

Her lips twisted into a cruel smile, and her eyes darkened, gleaming with malice. "Thank you," she whispered, her voice suddenly cold and mocking. "My hero."

Before he could pull away, her body shifted, the soft silk of her kimono dissolving into strands of thick, gleaming silk. Her legs elongated grotesquely, transforming into the spindly legs of a massive spider, her torso merging with the swollen abdomen that shimmered darkly in the dim light.

The man screamed, but it was too late. The jorōgumo's spider legs shot out, pinning him against the wall with terrifying speed. Thin strands of webbing coiled around his body, binding his arms and legs, lifting him off the ground as he struggled helplessly.

The jorōgumo cackled, her once-beautiful face twisting into a grotesque mask of cruelty. "Don't ssstruggle," she hissed, her voice dripping with malice. "You'll only make it worssse."

The man's eyes widened in terror as he looked around the alley. To his horror, he saw that he wasn't the only one. Other victims were cocooned in webbing, their bodies limp, their faces pale as they hung helplessly from the walls and ceilings of the alleyway. The jorōgumo had been busy.

With one final, heart-wrenching scream, the man was silenced, his body wrapped tightly in the jorōgumo's silken threads. The alley fell silent once more, the only sound the faint rustle of the jorōgumo's legs as she skittered back into the shadows, awaiting her next victim.

後見

Wakamono moved swiftly through the streets, his heart pounding in his chest. The cries of terror and the chaotic sounds of battle echoed all around him, but here, in this part of the city, there was an eerie stillness. Something was wrong.

As he approached an alley, a strange sensation prickled at the back of his neck, an instinct he had learned to trust. He slowed his pace, his eyes narrowing as he scanned the darkened street. And then he heard it.

"Help... please..."

The voice was faint, barely audible over the distant noise of the city. Wakamono's grip tightened on the hilt of his katana, his senses on high alert. The voice was too soft, too rehearsed.

He stepped into the alley cautiously, his movements deliberate as he followed the sound. As he rounded the corner, he saw her—a young woman, trembling, her kimono torn, leaning against the wall. She looked up at him with wide, tear-filled eyes, her face pale and streaked with dirt.

"Please... help me..." she whispered, her voice trembling.

Wakamono's eyes narrowed, his gut churning with unease. It must be a trap. He started to take a step backward—

The woman's lips twisted into a dark smile, and her eyes gleamed with malice. In a blink, her form began to shift, elongating into the hideous shape of the jorōgumo, her body transforming into that of a massive spider.

Wakamono leaped back, his katana drawn in an instant. He cursed under his breath.

The spider-woman cackled, her voice echoing eerily through the alley. "Oh, a Kōken," she hissed, her voice dripping with mockery. "How fun."

Wakamono's heart pounded as he prepared himself for the fight. The alley was narrow, and the jorōgumo's webs were already everywhere. He could see the glinting threads catching the faint light, strung across the walls and ceiling like a trap ready to snap shut. Worse, there were others—people, still cocooned in the webbing, their bodies limp and appearing lifeless.

Wakamono took a steadying breath. This wasn't just a fight against a spirit—this was a rescue mission. He had to be smart, had to be quick.

The jorōgumo lunged.

Her grotesque spider legs sliced through the air with deadly precision. Wakamono barely managed to dodge, the sharp limbs grazing his side as he twisted out of the way. A sharp pain flared where the jorōgumo's leg had caught him—a minor cut, but deep enough to slow him down.

He gritted his teeth, gripping his katana tightly as he sidestepped, keeping his eyes on the monstrous figure before him. The alley was too narrow, the webs too thick. The jorōgumo was faster than him here, her movements quick and fluid as she skittered over and between the walls.

Wakamono's mind raced. He had fought spirits before, but the jorōgumo was different. Her strength wasn't just her physical self—it was in the way she controlled the space, the way her webs turned the alley into a trap. Every movement Wakamono made had to be precise, deliberate. He couldn't afford any mistakes.

The jorōgumo cackled, her voice echoing through the alley as she circled him. "You're bleeding," she hissed, her eyes gleaming with malicious glee. "Ss-soon, you'll be just like them."

She gestured with one of her long, spindly legs toward the cocooned figures hanging from the walls, their bodies limp and pale. Wakamono's stomach churned as he saw the bite marks on their exposed flesh, the faint discoloration of their skin from the jorōgumo's toxic bite. She hadn't drained them completely, yet, but it was clear they were close to death.

Wakamono forced himself to stay focused, his katana raised. The pain in his side was sharp, but he could still fight. He had to.

The jorōgumo lunged again, faster this time, her fangs bared as she struck. Wakamono sidestepped, slashing with his katana, but she was too quick. Her legs tangled with his, pulling him off balance. He stumbled, his back slamming into the wall as the jorōgumo advanced, her webbing glistening in the dim light.

"Relax. Make this easier on yourssself," she sneered, her voice low and mocking.

Wakamono's pulse raced. His side throbbed with pain, and he felt the web threads sticking to his skin and clothes, slowing him down. The alley was a trap, but he couldn't retreat. Not with those people still hanging in her web.

His thoughts flashed back to Red Mist's teachings. Patience, focus—wait for the right moment.

The jorōgumo lunged again, her fangs snapping toward him. This time, Wakamono didn't dodge. Instead, he shifted his weight, driving his katana upward as the jorōgumo's body descended. His blade found purchase in her abdomen, and the creature screeched in agony as dark ichor spilled from the wound.

She recoiled, her legs flailing as she tried to pull away from him, but Wakamono pressed forward, driving his blade deeper. The jorōgumo's human half contorted violently, her face twisting with rage and pain.

For a moment, Wakamono thought he had her. But just as quickly, she twisted her body, wrenching herself free from his blade. She skittered back, her eyes filled with fury.

"You're a fool," she spat, her voice trembling with hatred. "But thisss isn't over."

Before Wakamono could respond, the jorōgumo darted into the shadows, disappearing down the narrow alley. Her form vanished into the darkness, leaving only the faint sound of her clicking legs as she fled.

Wakamono staggered back, his side burning with pain. He wanted to chase her, to finish the fight, but his gaze shifted to the hanging victims—the people still trapped in her web. Their faces were pale, their bodies weakened by the poison coursing through them.

He didn't have a choice.

Sheathing his katana, Wakamono approached the nearest cocooned figure, his heart heavy. He carefully drew his knife, cutting through the thick strands of web that bound them. The victim's body slumped into his arms, weak but still breathing.

Wakamono worked quickly, freeing the others from the web one by one. The poison had weakened them, but they were alive. As he cut through the last of the webs, his breath came in ragged gasps, the pain in his side growing sharper.

He had barely finished when a familiar sound echoed through the alley.

"*I see you.*"

Wakamono froze, his heart skipping a beat. The voice was soft, chilling—too familiar. His pulse quickened as he scanned the alley, but there was no one there.

The words echoed again, clearer this time. "*I see you.*"

His chest tightened. He had heard those words before, in his nightmares, and now they followed him into the waking world. But there was no time to dwell on the ominous message. The victims were freed and Wakamono had to heal his own seeping wounds.

Wakamono's breath came in ragged gasps as he stood in the now-silent alley, his body still tense, his side burning from the jorōgumo's strike. He drew his healing blade and plunged it into himself, wincing at the momentary pain.

"*I see you.*"

His heart pounded in his chest, the cold grip of fear winding through him. He clenched his fists, his gaze darting around the alley, searching for something—anything—that might explain the voice. But the narrow street was empty, save for the unconscious victims at his feet.

His frustration boiled over.

"Where are you?" Wakamono shouted, his voice raw with desperation and anger.

For a moment, there was nothing. Just the stillness of the alley, the distant sounds of chaos from the city, the faint rustling of the wind.

Then, the ground trembled beneath him.

Wakamono's eyes widened as the tremor grew stronger, the cobblestones cracking underfoot. The walls of the alley shook, dust and debris falling from the rooftops as the violent tremors increased in intensity. The air seemed to thicken with an oppressive weight, pressing down on him like an invisible force.

And then, a voice—a deep, rumbling voice that seemed to rise from the very depths of the earth—answered him.

"Here."

The word resonated through the ground, vibrating in Wakamono's bones, filling the air with a dark, malevolent energy. He felt his pulse quicken, fear gnawing at the edges of his mind.

Wakamono spun toward the source of the voice, his heart racing. The ground beneath him cracked and split, jagged lines of destruction tearing through the streets, snaking their way toward the marketplace.

He bolted out of the alley, his katana gripped tightly in his hand, his eyes wide with fear and determination. As he reached the end of the narrow street, the scene before him took his breath away.

The marketplace—the once-bustling heart of Sanpuku—was now in ruins. Stalls lay overturned, debris scattered everywhere. The ground was split wide open, deep fissures cutting through the earth. Smoke rose from the cracks, and the air was thick with the scent of burning.

In the center of it all, the ground continued to shake, a massive rupture forming as the earth groaned and buckled. The cracks grew wider, spreading out like veins across the ruined marketplace.

Wakamono stood frozen, his breath caught in his throat.

Something was coming.

10.

THE ANCIENT CEMETERY LOOMED before Red Mist, shrouded in fog and silence. Cracked gravestones jutted from the ground like broken teeth, weathered by time and neglect. The air was heavy with decay, and the faint scent of damp earth clung to the mist that swirled at her feet.

Red Mist moved cautiously through the overgrown path, her katana ready at her side. She could feel the presence of the malevolence she sought—something watching her from the shadows. The air was thick with tension, the kind that set her instincts on edge.

She passed the old temple at the edge of the cemetery, its once-grand entrance now reduced to little more than crumbling pillars. The temple had been abandoned for years, but the spirits that lingered here had not left. It was a place where the living dared not venture, and for good reason.

A soft rustling sound broke the stillness, and Red Mist's eyes narrowed as she moved toward the source. Her senses were sharp, trained to detect even the faintest disturbance. She stepped lightly over the uneven ground, her breathing steady, her mind clear.

As she approached the heart of the cemetery, she saw it—perched on a crumbling tombstone, watching her with glowing, malevolent eyes.

It was no ordinary cat. Its two tails swished lazily behind it, each movement unnaturally fluid. The creature's fur was as black as the shadows it inhabited, blending seamlessly into the darkened surroundings. But it was the eyes—those glowing, ember-like eyes—that sent a chill down Red Mist's spine.

The nekomata let out a low, guttural hiss, its sharp fangs glinting in the dim light. With one graceful leap, it bounded off the tombstone and disappeared into the mist, its movements quick and elusive.

Red Mist tightened her grip on her katana and followed.

As she moved deeper into the cemetery, the ground trembled beneath her feet. She stopped, her senses heightened, as the ground began to shift and crack. Thin, skeletal hands burst through the soil, clawing their way to the surface.

The dead were rising.

With a swift, practiced motion, Red Mist unsheathed her katana and spun, slicing through the brittle bones of the first skeleton to emerge. It collapsed into a pile of dust and bone fragments at her feet, but already, more were clawing their way free from the graves.

The nekomata was playing its game, toying with her by raising the dead.

Red Mist moved swiftly, her blade flashing in the mist as she cut down the undead one by one. The skeletal figures lunged at her, their bony hands reaching out, but her strikes were precise, her movements fluid. She didn't slow, her mind focused on the task at hand.

But no matter how many she destroyed, more kept coming. The nekomata's power was strong here, and the dead seemed endless.

The cat spirit reappeared, darting between the gravestones, its glowing eyes watching her every move. It hissed again, and as it did, another wave of corpses rose from the earth, their hollow eye sockets trained on Red Mist.

She gritted her teeth and pressed forward, her blade slicing through the horde of undead. Bones shattered under her strikes, but the battle was taking its toll. The dead seemed endless, and the nekomata was toying with her, staying just out of reach, raising more corpses with every step she took.

The ground beneath Red Mist's feet continued to tremble as more skeletal hands clawed their way through the earth. She swung her katana in a wide arc, slicing through a pair of skeletons that lunged at her from the haze. Bones shattered and clattered to the ground, but for every skeleton she cut down, two more seemed to rise.

Her breath was steady, controlled, but the sheer number of the dead was overwhelming. The cemetery had turned into a battlefield, and the nekomata watched from the shadows, its glowing eyes gleaming with twisted amusement. The spirit cat perched on a distant gravestone, flicking its two tails lazily as it summoned more corpses to rise from their resting places.

Red Mist moved with precision, her katana flashing through the dim light as she cut down the skeletal figures. They were brittle, their bones weak from decay, but their numbers were endless. She could feel the ground shifting beneath her with every strike, as though the very earth were rebelling against her presence.

A skeletal figure lunged at her from behind, its bony fingers outstretched, but Red Mist spun, her katana slicing through its ribcage in one clean motion. The skeleton crumbled, its bones falling to dust at her feet. She pressed forward, her eyes locked on the nekomata, who remained just out of reach, always retreating deeper into the cemetery.

The dead rose again, their bones clattering as they reassembled, their hollow eyes fixed on Red Mist. She gritted her teeth and swung her katana with renewed force, the blade flashing through the mist as it severed limbs and shattered skulls. Each strike was precise, calculated, but the nekomata was wearing her down, forcing her to expend energy on the endless tide of undead.

Red Mist dodged a skeletal arm that swung at her from the left, her movements graceful despite the chaos around her. She countered with a swift upward slash, severing the arm at the elbow before driving her katana through the ribcage of another skeleton that lunged from the side. She had to keep moving—staying still meant death.

But the dead just kept coming.

She felt a surge of frustration as she cut down another wave of skeletons. The nekomata was playing with her, raising more corpses to distract her, to tire her out. She couldn't afford to let it gain the upper hand, but the dead were relentless.

A sudden chill swept through the air, and Red Mist's eyes narrowed as she sensed something darker approaching. One of the graves to her right erupted with a burst of energy, and from it emerged a hulking figure—larger than the others, its bones thick and cracked. The skeletal giant let out a deep, echoing crunch as it rose to its full height, towering over the gravestones.

Red Mist's heart pounded as the giant skeleton lumbered toward her, its massive arms swinging with deadly force, indiscriminately swatting away its boney brethren. She leaped backward just in time, the skeletal fist slamming into the ground where she had stood, sending a shockwave through the earth. The impact cracked the nearby gravestones, scattering debris across the cemetery.

The nekomata hissed from its perch, its eyes glowing brighter as it reveled in the chaos. Red Mist knew she had to end this—she couldn't keep fighting the dead forever.

With a burst of speed, she dashed toward the skeletal giant, dodging its massive swings as it tried to crush her. Her katana flashed through the air, slicing through the giant's ribs and shoulder, but it barely slowed the creature. Its bones were thick, harder to break than the smaller skeletons she had been fighting.

Red Mist darted behind the giant, her blade cutting through its spine with a powerful strike. The giant let out a low groan as its bones cracked, and with a final swing of her katana, she severed its head from its body. The massive skull crashed to the ground, thudding against the upturned soil as the rest of the skeleton collapsed in a heap of bones.

Panting, Red Mist turned her attention back to the nekomata. The cat spirit let out a low hiss, its tails flicking in irritation as it realized she had destroyed its most powerful servant. It was time to end this.

Red Mist pressed forward, her katana raised as she advanced on the nekomata. The dead still stirred around her, but their movements had slowed as the cat lost its focus. The nekomata darted between the gravestones, but Red Mist was faster.

With a burst of speed, she cornered the cat spirit near the edge of the cemetery, her blade ready to strike. The nekomata crouched low, its glowing eyes narrowing as it hissed at her, but Red Mist was prepared.

Just as she was about to strike, a voice called out from the shadows behind her.

"Here, kitty, to mama."

The voice was soft and sweet, almost playful, but it sent a cold chill down Red Mist's spine. She froze, her katana poised mid-strike as the nekomata's eyes gleamed with sudden recognition.

Red Mist turned, her heart pounding, and there, standing in the fog, was Yama-uba.

The old crone's eyes twinkled with a strange, eerie light as she stepped forward, her hand outstretched toward the nekomata. "Come now, little one," she cooed. "You've had your fun."

The nekomata let out a low purr and slinked away, darting into the thick haze at Yama-uba's call. Red Mist watched in frustration as her target slipped away, disappearing into the shadows.

Yama-uba's lips curled into a smile as she looked at Red Mist, her eyes gleaming with dark amusement. "That was close," she said, her voice dripping with false praise.

Red Mist lowered her katana, her gaze wary but steady. "What do you want, Yama-uba?" she asked, her voice calm despite the tension in the air.

Yama-uba chuckled softly, the sound sending another shiver down Red Mist's spine. "I know something that may interest you," she said, her tone light but with an underlying menace. "For your young apprentice... death approaches."

Red Mist's eyes narrowed, her grip tightening on her sword. "What are you talking about?"

Yama-uba's smile widened. "You and the boy... fated to perish together," she said, her voice lilting like a song. "Make haste. The darkness comes for you both."

Red Mist's heart raced, but she didn't let it show. She took a step forward, her expression hardening. "If you know something, tell me."

But Yama-uba only shook her head, her eyes gleaming with amusement. A slight cackle crept from her malicious smile.

With that, Yama-uba turned and melted into the mist, her form dissolving as quickly as it had appeared. The cemetery fell silent once more, the eerie stillness settling over the gravestones.

Red Mist stood alone, her mind racing with Yama-uba's words. Wakamono... in danger. The darkness was coming.

She had to find him.

THE AIR WAS THICK with ash and smoke, the remnants of the marketplace scattered in every direction. Wakamono stood at the edge of the ruined square, his chest rising and falling in shallow, panicked breaths. Beneath his feet, the ground continued to tremble—slow, methodical tremors that felt like the heartbeat of something vast and ancient stirring beneath the surface.

The fissure at the center of the marketplace widened, the cracks splitting open like a wound that refused to close. A low, deep rumble rose from the depths, vibrating through the ground, rattling the stones beneath his feet. Wakamono's heart pounded in his chest, and despite every instinct screaming at him to run, he couldn't move.

A terrible pressure bore down on him, pressing into his lungs, choking the breath from his throat. It wasn't just fear—this was something darker, something sinister. The weight of it felt like an invisible hand wrapping around his chest, squeezing tighter with each passing second.

And then, with a thunderous crack, the ground split fully open.

At first, all Wakamono saw was darkness—an abyssal void opening in the earth, belching out thick, acrid smoke. But as the smoke cleared, a massive clawed hand, dripping with black, corrosive sludge, emerged from the fissure and slammed into the street. The ground hissed and bubbled where the liquid touched, leaving deep, smoldering scars on the earth.

The claw was followed by another, each finger ending in jagged, talon-like points that seemed to carve into the ground as they rose. Slowly, agonizingly, the rest of the figure emerged—a hulking, twisted form, broad and hunched, covered in jagged, charred scales that shimmered with a dull, hellish glow. The scales were uneven, cracked, like a body forged in fire and left to rot.

Wakamono's breath hitched in his throat as he looked up—higher and higher—until he saw the demon's face.

Onkai's head was massive, his features grotesque and twisted, as though pain itself had shaped his visage. His eyes—burning embers set deep into a skull-like face—blazed with an unnatural, insatiable hunger. They burned not just with hatred, but with something darker—delight, pleasure. His lips, if they could be called that, pulled back into a smile that was more a sneer, jagged and blackened teeth visible beneath.

But it wasn't the physical appearance that filled Wakamono with terror. It was the overwhelming presence. The sheer malevolence that radiated from the demon made it hard to breathe, as if the air around him was thickening into something solid, something suffocating. Wakamono felt his knees weaken, the strength in his legs faltering, his mind screaming at him to flee—but his body refused to obey.

Onkai rose fully from the fissure, his towering form casting long, jagged shadows over the ruined marketplace. His chest rumbled with each breath, deep and steady, like the sound of distant thunder. His massive arms stretched outward, each movement slow and deliberate, as though he was savoring his release from the depths.

Wakamono's heart pounded in his ears, his fingers twitching as he reached for his katana, but his hands shook uncontrollably. He had faced spirits, beasts, even powerful oni before. But this—this was different. This was some ancient evil, something primal.

Onkai's head turned slowly, his burning eyes finally settling on Wakamono.

A chill raced down Wakamono's spine as the demon's gaze pierced him, locking him in place. It felt as though those eyes saw into his very soul, stripping him bare, exposing every fear, every doubt. The pressure grew unbearable, the weight of the demon's presence pressing down on him like a suffocating shroud.

For a long, agonizing moment, Wakamono couldn't breathe.

Then, Onkai's chest rumbled, and a low, guttural growl echoed from deep within the demon's throat. His massive body shifted, the scales scraping and cracking as he moved, each sound sending a jolt of fear through Wakamono's bones.

The ground itself seemed to groan under Onkai's weight, the cracks spreading further as the demon took a step forward. His massive, clawed foot slammed into the ground, sending shockwaves rippling outward, the space beneath Wakamono trembling violently.

The demon's head tilted slightly, his burning gaze never leaving Wakamono. There was no rush, no haste in his movements. Onkai was savoring the moment—the fear, the pain that radiated from the city, the suffering of the spirits and souls scattered throughout.

Wakamono's throat tightened, his mind racing, but all he could do was stare. Stare at the monstrous figure towering before him, at the embodiment of pain and suffering that had crawled its way from the depths of the earth.

And in that moment, as Onkai's shadow loomed over him, Wakamono felt something he hadn't felt in a long time.

Hopelessness.

The marketplace trembled beneath Onkai's massive form, the air thick with the acrid stench of burning rock and sulfur. Wakamono's chest heaved, each breath a struggle as the weight of the demon's presence pressed down on him. His hand tightened around the hilt of his katana, but his fingers trembled with fear.

Onkai's burning eyes remained fixed on Wakamono, and though the demon had yet to strike, the anticipation of pain was almost worse than the blow itself. Onkai wasn't in a hurry. He was savoring the moment, enjoying the fear that wafted off Wakamono like heat from a dying fire.

Wakamono gritted his teeth, trying to steady his shaking hands. He had faced danger before, but nothing like this. Onkai was more than just a physical threat—he was a living embodiment of suffering, and the malevolent energy that surrounded him gnawed at Wakamono's resolve.

With a low, rumbling growl, Onkai finally moved. His massive, clawed hand shot forward, faster than Wakamono could have anticipated. The blow was more of a swipe than a strike—deliberately pulling its power back, as if Onkai was holding himself back to toy with his prey.

Wakamono barely managed to duck under the massive claws, his heart racing as the force of the swipe sent a gust of wind whipping through the ruined marketplace. He rolled to the side, coming up on one knee, his katana raised.

Before he could catch his breath, Onkai swung again—this time with more force. Wakamono threw himself backward, barely avoiding the strike, but the shockwave from the impact sent him stumbling. Onkai's claws slammed into the ground, sending a spray of dirt and debris flying into the air.

The demon chuckled—a deep, rumbling sound that reverberated through the ground. "Do you feel it, boy?" Onkai's voice was low, almost taunting. "The pain... the fear... it's delicious."

Wakamono's jaw clenched. He knew Onkai was enjoying this—relishing in the torment, stretching out the battle just to watch him squirm. But he couldn't let that stop him. He had to fight back. He had to do something.

With a burst of speed, Wakamono dashed forward, his katana flashing as he swung at Onkai's exposed side. The blade struck the demon's charred scales with a sharp clang, but the impact barely left a scratch. Onkai's body was like stone—impenetrable, invulnerable.

The demon didn't even flinch.

Instead, Onkai's head turned slowly toward Wakamono, the burning embers of his eyes narrowing. His lips twisted into a smile—a cruel, mocking grin that sent a chill racing down Wakamono's spine.

"Is that all?" Onkai growled, his voice dripping with disdain.

Wakamono staggered back, his breath coming in ragged gasps. His katana had done nothing—barely a scratch on Onkai's scales. The realization hit him like a punch to the gut. How was he supposed to fight something like this?

Onkai moved again, this time slower, more deliberate. He wasn't in a rush. He didn't need to be. Wakamono was no threat to him, and he knew it. The demon's claws dragged along the ground, carving deep furrows into the earth as he circled Wakamono like a predator toying with its prey.

Wakamono's mind raced, searching for a plan, for something—anything—that could turn the tide of the battle. But Onkai's presence was suffocating, crushing his thoughts under the weight of despair. Every step the demon took sent tremors through the ground, each one a reminder of the overwhelming power Wakamono was up against.

And then, with terrifying speed, Onkai struck again.

His massive clawed hand came down toward Waka-mono, a blur of jagged scales and oozing black sludge. Wakamono barely had time to react, diving to the side as the demon's claws slammed into the ground, missing him by inches. The force of the impact sent a shockwave rippling through the earth, throwing Wakamono off balance.

He hit the ground hard, his body aching from the impact. Gritting his teeth, he scrambled to his feet, only to see Onkai already closing in.

The demon's laughter echoed through the marketplace, a low, menacing sound that made Waka-mono's blood run cold. "You can't hurt me, boy," Onkai growled, his voice filled with dark amusement. "But I can hurt you."

Before Wakamono could react, Onkai's clawed hand swung out in a wide arc, catching Wakamono across the chest. The blow wasn't meant to kill—it was meant to hurt. Pain exploded through Waka-mono's body as he was sent flying through the air, crashing into the rubble of a nearby stall.

His katana slipped from his grasp as he hit the ground, the impact knocking the wind out of him. He gasped for breath, his vision swimming as pain radiated through his chest. Every breath was a struggle, the sharp pain of the blow making it feel like his ribs had been shattered.

Onkai's heavy footsteps echoed in the ruined square as he approached, each step sending tremors through the ground. Wakamono struggled to push himself up to a knee, his arms trembling with the effort, but the pain in his chest made it impossible to move.

The demon loomed over him, his eyes glowing with twisted delight. "You see, now," Onkai rumbled, his voice soft but filled with dark pleasure. "Pain is the only truth."

Wakamono gritted his teeth, his body shaking with pain, but his mind was still focused. He couldn't give up. Not now. Not yet.

Wakamono's chest heaved as he struggled to push himself up from the rubble, his arms trembling under the weight of his own pain. Each breath was a sharp reminder of the blow he'd taken, the dull ache in his ribs making it difficult to think, let alone move. His katana lay just out of reach, glinting in the dim light as dust swirled in the air.

Onkai stood over him, watching with those burning, hate-filled eyes. The demon's hulking form seemed to pulse with dark energy, each breath he took a slow rumble that shook the very ground beneath them. Wakamono could feel the malice radiating from Onkai—the sheer delight the akuma took in his suffering.

For a moment, Wakamono lay still, his mind racing, trying to piece together a plan. But nothing came. The demon was too strong, too fast, too impervious to the attacks Wakamono had tried. Every instinct screamed at him to run, to find safety, but there was none.

He couldn't run.

Not now. Not with the city in ruins. Not with so many lives at stake.

Gritting his teeth, Wakamono forced himself to his knees, the sharp pain in his chest making him wince. His hand reached out, grasping the hilt of his katana, fingers curling around the familiar weight of the weapon. He could feel his strength returning—slowly, painfully—but it was enough to lift himself back to his feet.

Onkai watched him, amusement flickering in those burning eyes. The demon didn't move. He didn't need to. Wakamono was nothing more than a toy to him—something to be played with, something to be broken.

With a low, defiant growl, Wakamono raised his katana, leveling the blade at the towering figure before him. His heart pounded in his chest, but his resolve had hardened. He wasn't going to let Onkai win. Not without a fight.

"Why?" Wakamono rasped, his voice hoarse but filled with anger. "Why are you doing this? Why Sanpuku? Why me?"

Onkai's twisted smile widened, a low chuckle rumbling from his chest. He took a slow step forward, his massive claws scraping against the ground. "Why?" the demon repeated, his voice dripping with mockery. "You seek answers, little Kōken?"

Wakamono tightened his grip on his katana, his jaw clenched in frustration. "Tell me," he demanded, his voice louder now, filled with desperation. "What is this all for?"

Onkai paused, his burning eyes narrowing slightly as he regarded Wakamono. For a brief moment, the air seemed to still, the tension thickening. Then, with a slow, deliberate movement, Onkai raised his clawed hand, pointing one talon directly at Wakamono's chest.

"Pain," the demon growled, his voice a low rumble. "Suffering. That is all there is."

Wakamono's pulse quickened. "What does that mean?"

Onkai's lips curled into a sneer. "You are not here for answers, boy. You are here to be broken."

Before Wakamono could respond, Onkai moved. His massive form blurred with terrifying speed as he closed the distance between them, his clawed hand sweeping toward Wakamono's midsection. Wakamono barely had time to react, raising his katana in a desperate attempt to block the strike.

The force of the blow sent shockwaves through Wakamono's arms, his bones rattling from the impact. He was thrown backward once more, crashing into the rubble behind him, his katana slipping from his grip again. Pain exploded through his side, and for a moment, the world spun in dizzying circles.

Onkai's laughter echoed through the ruins, the sound dark and twisted. "You thought you could fight me," he growled, his voice filled with derision. "You are nothing, little Kōken."

Wakamono gasped for breath, his vision swimming as he tried to push himself upright. But the pain was overwhelming—sharp, unrelenting—and his body refused to obey.

He was losing.

Onkai loomed over him, his shadow stretching long over the ruined square. "You want answers?" the demon sneered, his voice thick with malice. "You are not ready for them. I will feed on your suffering and I will take what I came for."

Wakamono's heart pounded in his chest, panic rising as he realized how close he was to the end. His mind raced, but there was no way out. Onkai was too powerful, and Wakamono was too weak, too broken.

Then, just as the despair threatened to consume him, a voice cut through the air—a voice that filled him with a sudden surge of hope.

"Wakamono!"

Her silhouette appeared on the edge of the ruins, her katana gleaming in the faint light as she charged toward the battlefield. Wakamono's chest tightened with relief, his heart swelling with renewed strength.

十二

WAKAMONO'S VISION BLURRED AS he lay on the
ground, his body aching from the brutal strikes. Pain
surged through his chest, each breath a struggle as
he tried to push himself up. His katana was still out
of reach, the weapon glinting faintly amid the rubble.
The weight of Onkai's presence pressed down on him,
suffocating and dark.

But then he heard her voice again—strong, steady,
and commanding.

"Wakamono!"

Red Mist.

Wakamono blinked through the haze of pain, lifting his head just enough to see her charging into the
fray. Her movements were fluid, graceful—every step
purposeful, every action precise. Her katana gleamed
in the dim light as she closed the distance between
herself and the towering demon.

Red Mist didn't hesitate. She moved like the wind,
her katana flashing as she struck at Onkai's side with
the full force of her skill. The blade connected with the

demon's charred scales, but instead of piercing flesh, the strike barely left a mark.

Onkai didn't even flinch.

Red Mist pivoted, her eyes narrowing as she swung again, aiming for a joint in the demon's armor-like hide. Her blade sliced through the air with deadly precision, but once again, it was as if she were striking stone.

The akuma's body was impervious.

Onkai's head turned slowly, his burning eyes now focused on Red Mist. There was no fear in his gaze—only amusement. He let out a low, rumbling chuckle that shook the ground beneath them, his mouth curling into that same twisted smile Wakamono had seen earlier.

Red Mist darted to the side, narrowly avoiding a swipe of Onkai's massive, clawed hand. She was fast—faster than Wakamono had been—and her movements were sharp, calculated. But no matter how many strikes she landed, no matter how expertly she moved, Onkai remained unscathed.

The demon swiped again, his claws raking through the air with terrifying speed. Red Mist dodged the attack, her body twisting gracefully as she moved out of his reach, the ground where his claws struck exploded in a cloud of dirt and debris. The force of the impact sent shockwaves rippling through the ruins, but Red Mist stayed on her feet, her eyes focused and unyielding.

Wakamono watched, his heart pounding in his chest. Red Mist was handling the fight better than he had, but even she couldn't break through Onkai's defenses. The realization gnawed at him, a sinking feeling in the pit of his stomach. If Red Mist couldn't hurt him... how could they win?

Onkai's laughter filled the air again, low and rumbling. "You're good," he growled, his voice dripping with dark amusement.

Red Mist's eyes narrowed, but she said nothing. Her grip tightened on her katana, and she moved again, launching into another attack. This time, she aimed for Onkai's legs, striking low, hoping to find a weakness in the demon's massive form.

But the result was the same.

Her blade connected with his armor-like scales, but the demon didn't react. His burning eyes gleamed with cruel satisfaction as he watched her movements, as if he were playing a game—waiting for her to tire, waiting for the moment he could strike back.

Wakamono struggled to push himself up, his arms trembling with the effort. The pain in his chest was sharp, each breath a reminder of the blow he'd taken. He couldn't lie here and do nothing. Not while Red Mist was fighting for her life. Not while the city was still in danger.

With a deep, painful breath, Wakamono forced himself to his knees. His vision swam for a moment, and he nearly collapsed back onto the ground, but he clenched his teeth and fought through the dizziness. He couldn't stop now.

Red Mist was still engaged in the fight, moving with precision, but Wakamono could see the strain beginning to show. No matter how hard she struck, Onkai didn't falter. The demon's laughter echoed through the ruins, each sound a taunt, a reminder of his dominance.

Wakamono's eyes flicked to his katana, lying just a few feet away, half-buried in the rubble. He had to reach it. He had to help her. Gritting his teeth against the pain, he crawled forward, his fingers brushing against the hilt of the blade.

His body screamed in protest, but he ignored it. Slowly, painfully, he rose to his feet, gripping the katana in his hand once more. His breath was ragged, his body weak, but his resolve had hardened. He wouldn't give up. Not yet.

As Red Mist dodged another of Onkai's swipes, Wakamono took a shaky step forward, his katana held tightly in his trembling hand.

The battle wasn't over.

The air crackled with energy as Wakamono took his place beside Red Mist, his chest heaving as he struggled to steady his breathing. The pain in his ribs still throbbed, but the sight of Red Mist—her calm focus, her unwavering stance—gave him strength. Together, they might stand a chance.

Onkai's towering form loomed over them, his burning eyes watching with amusement. The demon's twisted grin widened as he took in the sight of the two Kōken preparing to face him. He raised one massive, clawed hand, beckoning them forward. "Come, little warriors," Onkai growled, his voice a low rumble. "I have more pain to give you."

Without hesitation, Red Mist darted forward, her movements a blur of speed and precision. Wakamono followed suit, his katana raised, determined to strike where Red Mist's attacks had failed. The two moved in unison, their blades flashing as they slashed at Onkai from opposite sides.

Red Mist's katana sliced toward the demon's legs, while Wakamono aimed for his torso, hoping to land a blow on the exposed joints between the jagged scales. But Onkai moved with terrifying speed for a creature of his size, his massive claws swiping through the air with deadly force.

Red Mist spun gracefully, dodging the demon's attacks with practiced ease. She feinted left, then struck low, her blade aimed for the back of Onkai's knee. But the demon's scales were too thick, too impervious, and the katana barely scratched the surface.

Wakamono gritted his teeth as he lunged forward, his katana slicing toward Onkai's side. The blade connected with a clang, but the demon didn't even flinch. It was like striking a wall of iron. Wakamono cursed under his breath, leaping back just in time to avoid a crushing blow from Onkai's claws.

Onkai's laughter echoed through the ruined marketplace, a deep, mocking sound that sent a chill down Wakamono's spine. "Is that all?" the demon sneered, his eyes gleaming with malice. "Now you're wasting my time, and I have an eternity."

Red Mist and Wakamono exchanged a glance—just a flicker of acknowledgment before they moved in tandem again. This time, Red Mist leaped into the air, her blade arcing down toward Onkai's head, while Wakamono charged low, aiming for the demon's legs.

The demon moved, but not fast enough. Red Mist's katana struck the side of his skull, sending sparks flying as the blade glanced off his hardened scales. Wakamono's strike connected with Onkai's leg, but again, it was like hitting stone. The impact rattled through Wakamono's arms and shoulders, but he didn't stop. He slashed again, his strikes growing more desperate, more furious.

Onkai barely reacted.

With a snarl, the demon swung his arm in a wide arc, forcing both Red Mist and Wakamono to leap back. The ground shook with the force of the blow, rubble scattering in all directions. Onkai's laughter filled the air again, dark and twisted.

Red Mist was quick to recover, her eyes narrowing as she assessed the situation. She moved with deadly precision, her blade a blur as she struck at Onkai's joints, searching for any weakness in his impenetrable armor. Wakamono followed her lead, his movements less graceful but no less determined.

They fought as one—Red Mist's experience guiding their attacks, Wakamono's determination driving him forward. But no matter how many times they struck, no matter how carefully they coordinated their attacks, Onkai remained untouchable.

The demon let out a low growl of annoyance as he swatted away another of Red Mist's attacks. His eyes burned with frustration, his lips curling into a sneer. "Enough," he rumbled, his voice like thunder.

Wakamono barely had time to react before Onkai's massive clawed hand shot out, slamming into Red Mist with terrifying force. The impact sent her flying across the ruins, her body crashing into the rubble with a sickening thud.

"Red!" Wakamono's heart lurched as he watched her fall, but he didn't have time to reach her.

Before he could take a step, Onkai's hand closed around him, the demon's massive claws gripping him like a vice. Wakamono gasped, the air forced from his lungs as the heat of Onkai's touch seared through his clothes, burning into his skin. The pain was immediate and overwhelming, a fiery agony that spread through his torso.

Onkai's eyes gleamed with cruel satisfaction as he lifted Wakamono off the ground, holding him effortlessly in his massive grip. The heat intensified, the burning sensation growing sharper, more unbearable with each passing second.

Wakamono's vision blurred, his body wracked with pain as the heat of Onkai's grip began to sear through him. His katana slipped from his hand, clattering to the ground below as the demon's laughter echoed in his ears.

"Your suffering has just begun," Onkai growled, his voice a dark promise.

13
+三

RED MIST MOANED AS she pulled herself from the rubble, her body aching from the force of Onkai's blow. Her vision swam for a moment, the world around her a blur of smoke and ruin. But when her eyes finally cleared, the sight before her sent a surge of adrenaline through her veins.

Wakamono was suspended in the air, gripped tightly in Onkai's massive claw. The demon's eyes blazed with cruel delight as he tightened his grip, the heat radiating from his hand so intense that it distorted the air around him. Wakamono's face was twisted in pain, his body writhing as the burning claws pressed into his flesh.

Red Mist's heart lurched, panic momentarily freezing her in place. She had never seen Wakamono so helpless, so vulnerable. Her katana was still in hand, but she hadn't found a way to harm Onkai. Every strike had been useless against the demon's impenetrable scales.

She couldn't let this happen. She couldn't lose Wakamono.

With a sharp breath, Red Mist pushed herself to her feet, her muscles body in protest. She had to act. She had to save him.

Onkai's twisted grin widened as he watched Wakamono struggle. "Scream for me," the demon growled, his voice thick with sadistic pleasure.

Wakamono's chest heaved, his breaths shallow and ragged as the heat and pressure intensified. His mind raced, panic flooding his senses. He couldn't breathe. The pain was overwhelming, his skin blistering under Onkai's burning grip. His katana had slipped from his hand, leaving him defenseless.

But then his hand brushed against something—the pack slung over his shoulder, the familiar shape of the broken katana inside.

The healing blade.

Desperation coursed through Wakamono as his fingers closed around the hilt. He had no other choice, no other defense. He had to act now.

With a surge of adrenaline, Wakamono drew the broken blade from his pack, his vision swimming from the pain. His grip tightened around the hilt as he raised it.

With a cry of desperation, Wakamono brought the weapon down across Onkai's wrist.

The blade connected with the demon's scales, but instead of shattering or bouncing off, something else occurred—something none of them had expected.

The blackened, jagged scales at Onkai's wrist began to shift, to soften, the charred armor-like skin transforming before their eyes. Healed. Flesh. The broken katana was undoing the very thing that made Onkai invulnerable.

Onkai's eyes widened, his burning gaze flicking down to his wrist in disbelief. The demon's grin faltered, replaced by confusion, then anger.

Wakamono, panting and still held aloft, stared in shock as the scales on Onkai's wrist transformed into exposed, raw flesh. The heat still burned at his skin, but now there was hope.

"Red!" Wakamono's voice was hoarse, filled with pain and desperation, but also with determination. "Here!"

Red Mist's eyes narrowed as she saw the change. She moved swiftly, her body reacting before her mind could process what had just happened. Her katana gleamed as she sprinted toward Onkai, her focus zeroing in on the vulnerable patch of flesh.

With a powerful thrust, Red Mist drove her katana deep into Onkai's wrist, the blade sinking through the newly healed skin like a knife through soft clay.

Onkai roared, his voice a thunderous cry that shook the ground and rattled the very air around them. His grip on Wakamono loosened, the demon's entire arm jerking back as he stumbled from the strike.

Wakamono felt the pressure around him release, and he fell to the ground, gasping for breath as he clutched his chest. The pain in his side was sharp, his skin still sizzling from Onkai's grip, but he had done it. He had found a way to hurt the demon.

Onkai staggered back, his massive form towering over them as he clutched his injured wrist. His eyes blazed with fury, the twisted grin now gone, replaced by a look of pure rage.

But Red Mist didn't falter. She stood between Onkai and Wakamono, her katana still gleaming with the demon's dark blood.

Onkai's roar echoed through the marketplace, his massive form looming over Wakamono and Red Mist. The demon's wrist bled from the unexpected strike, but he was far from defeated. The battle had shifted, but Wakamono's body told a different story.

Wakamono stumbled to his feet, clutching the healing blade tightly in his hand. His skin was blistered and raw, the deep burns left by Onkai's grip still throbbing with searing pain. His chest was a patchwork of red, inflamed flesh, the heat from the akuma's touch having ravaged his body. Each movement sent waves of agony through him, his muscles screaming in protest.

Red Mist cast a glance at him, her face tight with concern. "Wakamono, you're injured. You shouldn't—"

"I must," Wakamono gasped, though his voice was strained with pain. He gritted his teeth, forcing himself to stand upright. "I can fight."

Red Mist didn't look convinced. The burns on his chest were severe—far worse than she had initially realized. His skin was blistered and charred, the telltale marks of Onkai's brutal grip etched into his flesh. It was a miracle he was still standing.

"Wakamono," Red Mist urged, her voice firm but gentle. "I can handle this."

But he shook his head, determination flashing in his eyes. "No. We do this together." His breaths were shallow, the pain overwhelming, but he wasn't going to give up. Not now. Not when they had finally found a way to hurt Onkai.

Red Mist hesitated, her eyes narrowing as she studied his injuries. She could see the pain etched into his face, the way his body trembled with every step. But she also saw the fire in his eyes—the same determination that had driven him this far. She couldn't stop him.

"Stay close," she said, her voice low but resolute. "And don't push yourself too hard."

Wakamono nodded, tightening his grip on the broken blade. His body was screaming for rest, for relief, but his mind was focused. They had found a weakness in Onkai's impenetrable armor. Now, they had to use it.

Onkai let out a low growl, his burning eyes flicking between the two Kōken. His massive claws flexed as he prepared to strike again, but this time, Wakamono and Red Mist were ready.

Wakamono moved first, though every step sent fresh waves of agony through his burnt skin. He ducked under Onkai's massive claw as it swiped toward him, his breath coming in ragged gasps. The heat from the akuma's touch still clung to him, the burns on his chest throbbing with each movement.

But he couldn't stop.

With a cry of effort, Wakamono raised the healing blade and brought it down across Onkai's forearm. The charred scales shifted, softening into raw, exposed flesh as the healing took hold.

Red Mist didn't hesitate. She moved like lightning, her katana flashing as she drove her blade into the freshly healed skin. The strike landed true, piercing deep into Onkai's arm. The demon howled in pain, the ground trembling beneath him as he stumbled back.

But Wakamono's body betrayed him. The exertion of the attack sent shockwaves through his burns, the pain so intense that it nearly brought him to his knees. His legs wobbled, and for a brief moment, his vision clouded with white sparks.

Red Mist caught the stumble, her eyes flicking toward him. "Wakamono, fall back! You're hurt!"

"I'm fine!" Wakamono gritted his teeth, his chest heaving. His burns were unbearable, but he forced himself to stay upright. He couldn't stop. Not yet.

Onkai's burning gaze fixed on him, the demon's eyes filled with fury. "You... will... suffer!" Onkai growled, his voice like thunder.

The demon lashed out, his massive claws tearing through the air with terrifying speed. Wakamono barely managed to dodge, his body moving on instinct alone. The burns on his chest screamed with every movement, but he pushed through the pain, his focus unwavering.

Red Mist moved in once more, her katana gleaming as she struck at Onkai's side. But the demon was faster this time. He swung his arm in a wide arc, forcing both of them to leap back. The ground shook with the force of the blow, sending debris scattering in all directions.

Wakamono gasped, struggling to catch his breath. His body was at its limit, the pain from his burns nearly unbearable. But he couldn't stop. He wouldn't stop.

Red Mist cast another glance at him, her face tight with concern. "You can't keep this up, Wakamono."

"I have to," Wakamono panted, though his voice was weaker now. His hand trembled as he raised the healing blade once more. "We can end this."

With renewed determination, the two of them moved together, Wakamono healing Onkai's scales while Red Mist struck at the vulnerable flesh. Onkai howled with fury, his massive body trembling as they landed strike after strike.

But the battle wasn't over. Onkai's strength was still formidable, and despite their strategy, he wasn't going down easily.

Wakamono's legs trembled, his body threatening to give out beneath him. The burns on his chest flared with each breath, his vision blurring from the pain. But he couldn't stop. Not now.

With a final surge of strength, Wakamono slashed across Onkai's chest, the healing blade leaving a streak of raw flesh in its wake. Red Mist followed up with a powerful strike, her katana sinking deep into the demon's flesh.

Onkai's roar of pain filled the air, louder and more furious than before. His massive form trembled, his movements growing more erratic as dark blood poured from his wounds.

They were winning. But the battle wasn't over yet.

Onkai's roars echoed through the ruins, his massive form battered and bleeding from the relentless attacks of Wakamono and Red Mist. The once-impenetrable scales of his body had been transformed into patches of raw, vulnerable flesh, but the demon still stood, defiant and dangerous.

Wakamono struggled to stay on his feet, his chest heaving with each painful breath. His burns throbbed, the skin blistered and raw from Onkai's earlier grip. Every movement sent fresh waves of agony through his body, but he refused to give in. Not yet.

Red Mist glanced at him, her eyes filled with concern, but Wakamono gave her a firm nod. They had to keep pushing. Onkai was on the defensive, retreating slowly, hurling debris at them in desperate attempts to keep them at bay.

The ground shook as chunks of stone and wood flew through the air, forcing Red Mist and Wakamono to dive for cover. Onkai's growls grew more frantic, his movements less precise. He was weakening, and they both knew it.

But Wakamono's strength was fading fast. His legs trembled, his vision tunneled, and his grip on the healing blade felt weaker with each passing second. He couldn't get close to Onkai—not like this. The pain was too much, his body too broken.

But there was one thing he could do.

With a surge of determination, Wakamono raised the healing blade, his eyes locking onto Onkai. The demon's massive form twisted, his movements sluggish as he retreated further. This was the moment—his only chance.

Gathering every ounce of strength he had left, Wakamono flung the healing blade.

The weapon sailed through the air, spinning end over end before striking the top of Onkai's head. With a soft thud, the blade bounced off, clattering to the ground below.

But the effect was instant.

The healing magic rippled across the top of Onkai's skull, and where the blade had struck, a patch of the demon's charred, armor-like scales softened into raw, exposed skin.

Onkai roared in fury, his hands clawing at his head, but it was too late. The weakness had been revealed.

Red Mist didn't hesitate. Her katana flashed in the dim light as she charged toward Onkai, her eyes locked on the small patch of exposed skin. The demon was too focused on the blade that had fallen at his feet to notice her approach.

As Onkai reached down to grab the healing blade, Red Mist leaped into the air, her katana raised high.

With a single, powerful strike, she drove the blade into the exposed spot on Onkai's head.

The katana sank deep into the demon's flesh, piercing through the raw skin and the bone beneath. Onkai's roar of pain was deafening, the sound reverberating through the ruins as his massive body convulsed.

Dark, viscous blood poured from the wound as Onkai staggered, his movements jerking and uncontrolled. His massive hands clawed at the ground, desperate for something to hold onto, but there was nothing.

The demon's roars grew weaker, his body trembling as flames began to lick at his charred skin. In seconds, Onkai's entire body ignited, the flames consuming him from the inside out.

Red Mist pulled her katana free and stepped back as the fire spread, engulfing the akuma in an inferno of dark flames. Onkai's massive frame buckled, his knees giving way as the fire consumed him.

The battle was over.

As Onkai's body burned, Red Mist turned, her eyes scanning the battlefield until they found Wakamono. He was slumped against a pile of rubble, his chest rising and falling in shallow breaths, his face pale from the pain.

Without hesitation, Red Mist rushed to his side, kneeling beside him as she placed a hand on his shoulder.

"Wakamono," she said softly, her voice filled with concern. "Stay with me."

Wakamono's eyes fluttered open, the pain in his chest making it hard to breathe. His body was spent, his burns severe, but a weak smile crossed his face. "Did we... ?"

Red Mist nodded, her expression softening. "He's gone."

She reached down and picked up the healing blade, the small weapon that had made all the difference. Onkai's body continued to burn behind them, the flames crackling as they consumed the demon's remains, hardening his deceased form into blackened stone.

十四

THE SUN HUNG LOW in the sky, casting a soft, gold-en light over the city of Sanpuku. The air was still, the streets quieter than usual, though the sounds of rebuilding echoed through the ruins. After the fierce battle against Onkai, the city was beginning to heal—its people working tirelessly to repair what had been lost. But the scars of the fight still remained, both in the city and in the people who had lived through it.

Wakamono stood beside Red Mist, his chest still aching from the internal injuries he'd sustained dur-ing the battle. His hands were steady as he hammered nails into the new doorframe, though every swing of the hammer sent a dull throb through his body. His skin, still raw and blistered from Onkai's fiery grip, stretched painfully as he moved, but Wakamono grit-ted his teeth and pushed through it.

Red Mist worked beside him, her own move-ments more measured than usual. Though her injuries weren't as severe as Wakamono's, the bruises and cuts from the fight were still visible on her arms and face. But as always, she remained composed, her focus unwavering as they repaired the damage done to the city.

The rhythmic pounding of the hammer echoed softly through the street, mingling with the distant sounds of carts and voices. It was a far cry from the chaos that had consumed the city just a week ago, when the demon Onkai had risen from the ground, unleashing destruction upon everything in his path.

Wakamono paused for a moment, leaning against the doorframe as he caught his breath. Sweat beaded on his brow, the exertion of the day weighing heavily on him. His body was still weak from the fight, and though he had healed considerably, every movement was a reminder of the cost of their victory.

"You should rest," Red Mist said, her voice calm but firm as she glanced over at him.

Wakamono gave her a wry smile. "I'll rest when we're done."

Red Mist raised an eyebrow but said nothing, returning to her work with quiet efficiency. Despite her calm exterior, Wakamono knew she was watching him closely, monitoring his every movement. He could feel her concern, though she didn't voice it. He was still recovering, and they both knew he was pushing himself too hard.

But Wakamono had never been one to back down from a challenge.

With a deep breath, he picked up the hammer once more, driving another nail into the wooden frame. The work was monotonous but satisfying—a welcome distraction from the lingering tension that still hung over the city. As they worked, the occasional passerby would nod in thanks, acknowledging the efforts of the Kōken who had saved them from the devastation.

The doorframe creaked as Wakamono drove in the final nail, a sense of accomplishment settling over him as he stepped back to admire their work. The worst of the damage had been repaired, though there was still much more to do. But for now, it was enough.

Just as Wakamono was about to step back and rest, a familiar voice called out from behind them.

"You two have been working hard," Mrs. Jin said with a warm smile as she emerged from her home, balancing a tray in her hands. "Come, take a break. You both look like you could use some food."

Wakamono turned and grinned as he saw Mrs. Jin approaching. She moved with the same gentle grace that had always made him feel welcome, her face bright despite the challenges the city had faced, and was still facing. She carried a tray of rice and tea, the steam rising in thin tendrils, carrying the scent of warmth and comfort.

Red Mist glanced at the tray, then back at Wakamono. "I think we've earned it," she said, her expression softening.

Wakamono wiped his brow, his body protesting the idea of sitting down, but the smell of rice and the thought of rest were too tempting to resist. "Alright, if you twist my arm," he said with a tired chuckle, leaning the hammer against the wall as he stepped forward.

Mrs. Jin's smile widened as she set the tray down on a nearby table. "You've done more than enough. You both deserve this and more." She gestured for them to sit, and Wakamono gratefully collapsed onto a wooden stool, his body aching with relief.

Red Mist sat beside him, her movements more controlled but no less tired. Though she maintained her usual air of calm, the exhaustion in her eyes was clear. The battle had taken a toll on them both, not just physically but mentally. But for now, they could rest, even if only for a short while.

"Mr. Jin says the market's picking up again," Mrs. Jin said as she poured tea into two cups, her hands steady and practiced. "People are coming back. Slowly, but they're coming back." There was a note of pride in her voice, and Wakamono couldn't help but feel a sense of hope in her words.

He picked up his cup of tea, the warmth seeping into his fingers, soothing the aches in his body. "That's good to hear," he said, taking a small sip. "The city's strong. It'll recover."

Mrs. Jin nodded, her expression softening as she handed them bowls of rice. "Sanpuku's been through worse. We're survivors. But I can't imagine where we'd be without you two. You saved us."

Wakamono shifted, a flicker of discomfort crossing his face. He wasn't used to praise, especially not after the destruction they had just witnessed. "We did what we had to," he said, glancing at Red Mist.

Red Mist remained silent, her eyes focused on the tea in front of her. Wakamono knew she wasn't one to bask in gratitude, but the weight of Mrs. Jin's words wasn't lost on her.

"You did more than that," Mrs. Jin said, her voice full of warmth. "We'll never forget it."

Wakamono took a deep breath, his chest tightening for a moment before he forced himself to relax. There was still so much to do, so many lingering threats. But in this moment, sitting in the calm of the Jins' home, he allowed himself to feel the peace that had eluded him for so long.

"Thank you," he said softly, offering Mrs. Jin a smile.

She smiled back, her eyes twinkling with kindness. "Now eat up. You'll need your strength."

Just as Wakamono and Red Mist were settling into their meal, a hurried voice broke the tranquility.

"Kōken! Kōken!" A young man came running down the street, his breath ragged, his face drawn with fear.

He stumbled to a stop in front of them, clearly exhausted from his sprint.

Wakamono set his bowl of rice down slowly, his gaze already sharpening. Red Mist shifted in her seat, her instincts immediately on alert.

"What's happened?" Red Mist asked calmly, though her body was already poised to act.

The young man gulped in air before speaking, his words tumbling out in a rush. "There's been another tsukumogami attack! It's at the east market—the spirit is causing chaos."

Red Mist's jaw tightened, and Wakamono exhaled heavily, already knowing what came next. Though Onkai had been vanquished, the remnants of his malevolent influence still lingered in the city, and tsukumogami were among the most troublesome spirits to deal with.

Wakamono pushed himself up from his seat, his body protesting the sudden movement. His burns still ached, and his muscles and bones were far from fully recovered, but there was no choice. Sanpuku still needed them.

Mrs. Jin watched with concern from the doorway, her hands folded over her apron. "I thought things would settle down after that demon was dealt with," she said quietly.

Wakamono glanced back at her, offering a small, reassuring smile. "We hoped the same," he replied, though there was a weariness in his voice. "But there are still some lingering spirits that need handling."

Red Mist stood beside him, her eyes steady and calm as she gathered her things. "It won't last forever," she added, her voice measured. "But until it's done, we'll be here."

The young man shifted nervously, clearly anxious for them to hurry. "We'd better go," Wakamono said, giving Mrs. Jin a brief nod of thanks. "We'll be back soon."

Mrs. Jin gave them a worried but understanding smile. "Take care of yourselves," she said, her voice gentle. "Sanpuku is lucky to have you both."

Wakamono offered her a final nod, then turned to Red Mist. As they began walking toward the east market, he muttered, "I just hope it's not another merchant's cart."

Red Mist's lips twitched slightly, but she remained focused. "Whatever it is," she replied, her tone serious, "we'll handle it."

Wakamono and Red Mist walked side by side through the narrow streets of Sanpuku City, their footsteps quiet against the worn cobblestones. Though the city was still in the process of rebuilding, there was a renewed sense of life in the air—shops re-opening, families returning to their homes, and people slowly piecing their lives back together after the devastation.

The two Kōken moved with purpose, their presence a silent reassurance to the citizens they passed. But even as they made their way toward the east market, Wakamono couldn't shake the dull ache in his chest—the reminder of the fight with Onkai, the cost of their victory.

"We've done a lot here," Wakamono said, his voice low as they walked. "But it feels like it's never enough."

Red Mist glanced at him, her expression as steady and composed as always. "That's the nature of our work," she replied. "There's always more to be done. But that doesn't mean what we've done isn't enough."

Wakamono nodded, though he still felt the weight of it all pressing down on him. But he knew Red Mist was right. They had fought hard, and the city was still standing because of it. That had to count for something.

As they reached the outskirts of the east market, Wakamono took a deep breath, steeling himself for whatever lay ahead. The familiar tension of battle settled in his chest, but this time, there was something different—something lighter.

He glanced at Red Mist and saw the same determination in her eyes. Together, they would face whatever came next. Together, they would protect the city, the mountain, and Seken, no matter how many spirits or creatures came their way.

They moved forward as one, the weight of their duty resting on their shoulders, but the bond they had forged made them stronger. No matter what lay ahead, they were ready.

END

Epilogue

DEEP WITHIN THE MOUNTAINS, hidden from the light of day, the cave of Yama-uba echoed with the sound of dripping water and the slow crackle of the fire that burned eternally in the center of the cavern. The shadows danced wildly across the stone walls, twisting and contorting with every flicker of flame, casting eerie shapes that seemed to watch and whisper.

Yama-uba sat hunched near the fire, her long, tangled hair draped over her face, obscuring her twisted features. Her hands twitched as they traced frantic patterns in the dirt at her feet. She muttered to herself in broken phrases, her voice rising and falling with unpredictable intensity.

"Onkai... Onkai, my sweet," she hissed, her lips pulling back in a grotesque smile that quickly twisted into a grimace of rage. "Such power... such pain... wasted!"

Her bony fingers clawed at the ground, leaving deep scratches in the dirt as she seethed with frustration. The two remaining akuma stood nearby, silent and unmoving, their monstrous forms watching their mistress with a mixture of wariness and impatience.

Yama-uba's voice grew shrill, her eyes gleaming with a dangerous light. "He had the blade in his grasp! The Kōken should be nothing but ash beneath our feet... yet he failed! He failed!" She punctuated the word with a sharp, jabbing motion, as if stabbing an invisible enemy.

Her body trembled with fury, but then, as quickly as the anger had come, it was replaced by a deep, unsettling calm. She straightened slightly, her gaze turning inward, her thoughts shifting to the object of her obsession.

"The healing blade..." she whispered, her voice now soft, reverent. "It is the key. It will be mine. With it, I will undo the damage... I will undo the Kōken... and we will rule over all."

Her fingers curled into fists, and she rocked back and forth, her eyes unfocused as she mumbled incoherent words. The fire flickered and dimmed as if responding to her dark thoughts, casting the cave into deeper shadow.

The two remaining akuma exchanged a glance but said nothing. They knew better than to speak when Yama-uba was in one of her moods. But even they could sense the shift—the growing desperation in their mistress. Onkai had been one of her most powerful warriors, and his defeat had shaken her.

Yama-uba's head snapped up suddenly, her eyes narrowing as she focused on the two akuma. Her erratic muttering ceased, and a cruel smile spread across her face.

"You," she said, her voice dripping with malice as she pointed a gnarled finger at them. "You will not fail me like Onkai did. No... you will bring me what I desire. The blade. The end of the Kōken."

The akuma stood taller, their hulking forms casting massive shadows across the cave.

Yama-uba's laughter rang out suddenly, a high-pitched cackle that echoed off the cave walls, sending chills down the spines of her remaining servants. "Fail me," she warned, her tone turning icy, "and you will know pain far worse than anything Onkai ever imagined."

Her eyes gleamed in the firelight, the madness in her gaze more pronounced than ever. "Go now," she whispered, her voice dropping to a low, menacing tone. "Go and bring me the healing blade... or do not return at all."

The fire flared up, casting a blinding light across the cave as the two akuma turned and vanished into the shadows, their monstrous forms disappearing into the darkness.

As their footsteps faded, Yama-uba returned to her muttering, her fingers tracing patterns in the dirt once more. But now, there was a gleam of something darker in her eyes—a promise of vengeance, a hunger that would not be sated until she had the healing blade in her grasp and the Kōken were nothing but memories.

"We'll have it," she muttered, glancing back toward the depths of the cave.